I0659450

THE VOYAGES OF RALF, Vol. 1

The Arc of Purchaser

R.M. Kozan

Fresh Blue Ink

Ottawa

Fresh Blue Ink

is an imprint of Fresh Blue Inc.
33 Jackson Court, Ottawa, ON K2K-1B6

FreshBlueInk.ca

Paperback ISBN: 978-0-9920119-2-5
Electronic book ISBN: 978-0-9920119-3-2

Cover illustration (c) 2020 Christina Cartwright

First edition: August 2020

For Lois

THE VOYAGES OF RALF, Vol. 1

The Arc of Purchaser

(A Philosophical Dissertation
on the Nature of the Cosmos
or, at Least, a Few Laughs)

Prologue

I n the beginning, was this universe. It was uniform and conformed to the laws of itself. Thus being law-abiding, it was kin to all other universes: unexceptional, and therefore not meriting a pay increase.

In that time, before His Coming, the cosmos was without the hope and joy of true spirituality. The populations of the myriad worlds that composed the then under-funded universe were missing that one critical yet elusive trait of enlightenment: a god-like apathy concerning one's immediate physical circumstances and the chances of being eaten by monsters.

And no one came into their presence to explain this strange and wonderful potentiality, until He.

At His Coming, the people were taken by surprise, and thus did not fully appreciate His heroic quest and idiom. Also, it was very early in the morning. And so, it came to pass, that upon His First Coming, He was deported.

Whence this occurred, the people of this fair and great universe grew despondent. But it was too late! He, that is, He had gone.

Only then did they grasp His true philosophy. An uproar swept through the universe, one like that which had never been seen, because uproars are heard. All life mourned the loss of His presence. But, alas, the cry cast upward pleading for His return went unheeded.

He, and I mean, He did not return.

The people of the blessed universe knew that they must not abandon all hope. They knew that they must bide their time and wait for His return. They waited, but He did not return. They waited some more. Still, He did not return. They waited even some more, and yet

He did not return!

It was by that time they began to feel somewhat deflated. The cosmic tale of their tragic existence seemed more concerned with delaying any resolution of their primordial suffering and conflicts so as to get renewed for another season, rather than just getting on with the story, and risk it coming to an end. They lost their hope for enlightenment, and the darkness of immortal melancholy soon tumbled in.

Only a portion of a portion of the people in that dark era still sought His return. But these brave folk could not pursue this ultimate sacred quest as most of them had been locked into life-long service contracts forcing them to deliver fast food to suburbanites by bicycle.

And yet, the hope remained. Would this magnificent and gracious Being return to usher in a new era of heroism and justice? Would they, indeed, in some future epoch when enlightenment gazed lustily upon the infinite cosmos (note: universe may not be entirely infinite, and may contain nuts), witness the return of He, a guy with an unusually short name and lots of strange ideas that people don't cotton to until long after He is publicly and thoroughly squashed by a large, dense object provided by, and used at the insistence of, the government of the day?

A millennium passed. He did not return.

But then, one day, Another was revealed.

Book 1. The Thing from Beyond the Tri-Galactic Area!

Send us your tone deaf,
your misshapen
your inarticulate
those cast aside for seeking
Peace, Harmony & Joy
May we open our hearts to welcome
the new
May we spread our arms to embrace
the beautiful
No matter their form

[Statue of Special Equanimity (plaque),
New West York]

Dramatis Personae

Anark 337 (android)
        Maintenance team, NOSFERATU

Snorg Ballesto (Ihnewian)
        Technician, NOSFERATU

Thom Berishu (Terran)
        Captain, NOSFERATU

Slaarp Cootez (Martian)
        Comm Officer, NOSFERATU

Swep Fetherhed (Martian)
        Helm Officer, NOSFERATU

Karp Quelfin (Meowite)
        Chief Navigator, NOSFERATU

Ralf (Terran)
    Science Officer (intern), NOSFERATU

Fis Sithis (Kduimlian)
        Ambassador to Ksath

Ragnor Trepaloof (Martian)
        Helm Officer, NOSFERATU

Pob Trook (Ejsaanon)
        Commodore, Space City C-0004

Chapter 1. Tension and Resolution at Trinae

"Now! Full power to the starboard thrusters!" bellowed Captain Thom Berishu at his helm officer, Ragnor Trepaloof, as the pirate ship on the viewscreen disgorged another torpedo, this time aimed at their aft fin. It was a near miss.

"That pirate doesn't want to give us our Ambassador back, and he's the only one who can save the peace process," noted Chief Navigator Karp Quelfin, handily stating the obvious for those who have just joined us. "And we can't out-run or out-gun them without our anti-grav units, which you, dear Captain, have so kindly given to the Dennoue natives for their supposed self-defence, but who knows, are now likely watching us die out here while they relax on their zero-g reclinatrons."

"Program this now," demanded Berishu of Trepaloof, handing him a datapod.

"But Captain," Trepaloof eyed him uncertainly, "Did you check it with the navitron simulator? If we hit that black hole's horizon..."

Overlooking the tete-a-tete between the Space Corps StarCraft NOSFERATU and the pirate ship, name unknown, were the Dennoue and Trinae, asteroid-dwelling civilizations which circled a monstrously large, but somehow somewhat tame, black hole.

"We can't cut and run!" snarled Quelfin. "We must fight like Martians! These pirates will think we're a bunch of Terrans, no offense Captain."

The Captain's attention was elsewhere.

"Initiate flight on my mark. Trep, you got Part 2 ready?"

"Yes sir," affirmed Trepaloof smoothly.

"Part 2? What is that?" questioned an agitated Quelfin.

"No time. Mark!" shouted the Captain.

The NOSFERATU pushed away from the confrontation, falling down the gravity well, manoeuvring along an arc towards the dim circular outline that implied the threshold of the black hole.

Their assailants assumed they were withdrawing, but this was not the case.

The NOSFERATU swung hard behind the black hole, skimming the critical region, its velocity rising rapidly. At the precise co-ordinates, as programmed in Part 2, with the ship now hurtling just shy of light speed, the multi-thread soft script the Captain and his Science Officer had cobbled together moments earlier now automatically performed a molecular displacement of their ambassador from the pirate ship, back to the NOSFERATU's ready room, at light speed, and simultaneously managed to send a ship-to-ship missile, at just sub-light speed, destroying the pirate ship in a very orange and fiery ball of fire before its swash-buckling occupants had a chance to realize their leverage against the Alliance was now resting safely on the NOSFERATU, and the Dennoue/Trinae system was, at long last, militarily and politically stable.

It would take the NOSFERATU some period of time to decelerate from its great speed without its antigrav units, but the Captain could engineer a reverse slingshot to get them back to a reasonable speed relative to the asteroid on which they had left their anti-grav units, now no longer needed by the Dennoue due to Captain Berishu's risky stratagem.

"Well another wild gambit worked out for you Captain. You never fail to impress!" Quelfin spat these words at the Captain while instead looking at the highly attractive and multi-talented Dr. Miranda Von Leggentrope, the Captain's longtime science officer and confidant.

The Captain was also looking at her, ignoring the

usual verbal dribblings of Quelfin, who he considered skillful but a pain in the arse. Instead, the Captain raised his coffee mug, and gave a toast in honour of his trusted science officer, and her plan to soon depart.

"Things won't be the same around here without you, Doctor. You've been completely invaluable. Saved us all more times than I can recount. But, as you say, there is a time to fight the entire cluster, and a time to move to the suburbs, so well, may your retirement neighbourhood have more infrared than gamma rays!"

"Kind words, Captain, and very much appreciated," she responded. "Your own ingenuity cannot be overstated, but I appreciate your generosity of spirit. Your heart has always been in the right place, and we have done beautiful things. I anticipate great things for you and the NOSFERATU."

The time had come for the NOSFERATU and its Captain to return to Mars to pickup a replacement science officer, and receive fresh orders.

Chapter 2. People Are Our Greatest Asset

Management underestimated him as a solid mid-career contributor. He worked quickly and optimistically. He respected the authority of his superiors, the top brass at Space Corps High Command. He was seen as conservative, a functionary and nonthreatening. He carefully managed risk taken, always with an eye on results.

Often, he was heard to mutter, "I must work harder. I must advance more quickly. I don't have much time left. I've only ten sols until I get my pension..."

He had worked hard in Space Corps, that military bureaucracy which guarded the grand confederation of many planets and beings which was called, perhaps over-optimistically, The Triang-Dromed-Way Alliance. He was fully and rigorously qualified for his position as Captain of the StarCraft NOSFERATU.

Throughout his long, arduous training for a career in Space Corps, he was never given an easy break, or allowed to slide through a course with a minimal amount of effort as so many of his elite and well-connected competitors did. The reason for this was that the Captain was a Terran.

Captain Thom Berishu of the StarCraft NOSFERATU was a Terran.

Many of the other citizens of the predominantly Martian Alliance held an insidious and unreasonably malign bias against Terran martianoids. This made it challenging for the average Terran to succeed in any venture beyond the atmosphere of their home planet.

Captain Berishu's StarCraft NOSFERATU had earlier set course for Space City C-0004, located in a null gravity point between Terra and Luna, where the Captain would meet Commodore Pob Trook, and obtain his new orders for the NOSFERATU. Now, the

4

NOSFERATU floated leisurely near C-0004, and awaited the return of its Captain.

Berishu crouched, centred atop a trendy but recklessly uncomfortable chair in Commodore Trook's office, waiting patiently while the news feed from a nearby screen exhibited well-dressed people screaming at each other:

"It's clear that the People's Party has been taken over by the inducements of the Supreme Purple Worm. Since when does a foreign worm come before martianoids?"

"Hold on! So your idea of 'people' is limited to martianoids? Clearly, the Progress Party is in the pocket of Terran financiers and foreign interests!"

"Special interest groups drive both your agendas! Only the Unity party knows who're the dividers in our system. Give you a little hint: it's not the Martians! Why can't you be more like us?"

"Now, please, let's focus on the question before us, gentle-beings," admonished the moderator. "Why would your party be the best to bring beauty back to our political system? Let's again start with the People's Party, and then move to the next panellist, please."

"Well, as the party in power, we know what is going on, and clearly the Progress Party is looking backwards and running on a treadmill, I mean, if they exercise at all!"

"Outrageous! Just an ugly statement from an ugly, backwards person."

"Sir Tetraham- you can't use that kind of language on this program. We have nestlings watching..."

"I'm sorry but it had to be said-"

"There is nothing you have to say!" interrupted the representative of the Unity Party. "Clearly the purpose of all the other parties is to sell us out to off-world interests! Only the Unity Party can bring us all together!"

"Bring us all to Martian hegemony you mean!"

"Better than Terran hegemony, and ruin! We need old-fashioned Martian values, not Terran terrorists!"

"Preposterous! Fighting for minority rights is not terrorism!"

"Trying to destroy the Martian way of life is an attack on the entire Alliance!"

"Maybe people are sick of your out-sized leverage on the Alliance. Maybe it is time for someone other than Martians to be heard."

"Yes, but not you!!" screamed the Unity Party representative.

Berishu ignored this usual preheated, re-election rhetoric, and turned instead to peruse the odd décor of his surroundings. One thing Berishu had learned over his many sols in Space Corps was that one could quite often accurately surmise the origins of an officer by considering the way his/her/their/its office was decorated.

Martians filled their offices with antique Martian furniture, and drowned all wall space with large, gold-framed sandscapes.

Terrans possessed little functional furniture, as they were usually paid very poorly, and used conservative colours, grey and dark grey throughout, as they were embarrassed with having been appointed to a position of any importance. Their main goal in decorating was to avoid offense.

Ihnewians preferred vivid reds and eye-blowing blues with slashes of fiery oranges. Sometimes they had space funk hop piped in.

The beings of the Bosun system were colour-blind, so tended toward random collections of clashing colours, overwhelmed by heavy horizontal stripes.

However, Trook's office was quite apart from the norm, anybody's norm. Pastel pinks and mellow yellows were haphazardly scattered in patches along the walls. Posters of glossy chrome cities nestled in slime-slicked jungles were also slapped, at varying angles, on those walls.

Berishu was stumped.

Surely, he thought, she must be a member of one of the minor races. Perhaps a Delaroug, a Zin, or a Meowite. The design of the chair on which he perched certainly implied a non-martianoid or perhaps even non-bipedal physical form...

Suddenly the solution entered the Captain's cerebrum: Commodore Trook was an Ejsaanon!

Chapter 3. The Medium Is the Message

Berishu clutched his stomach, and held his tongue fast to the roof of his mouth.

"Ah Aron..." Berishu moaned as he struggled to control the sudden turbulence within his stomach (Editor's note: Aron, aka Celestial Acceptor of Late Fees and All-Mighty Guarantor of Authenticity, is the sole deity in the Alliance's primary religion, Aronism).

The door behind the desk turned, and Trook rolled in.

Great Aron, a Terran! That's all I need today, she thought. Outwardly, she decreased her frontal olfactory organ to show courtesy, and glided to her desk where she inserted one glistening tentacle into her translation apparatus.

A terrible smell filled the air, and lights on the translator box flickered for a moment before a simulated Martian voice emanated.

"Captain Berishu, I want to congratulate you on your last mission. I heard you did an exemplary job. That was the Dennoue-Trinae peace talks, is that correct?" As Pob Trook gurgled on, another of her tentacles oozed forward, sought out, and briefly shook Berishu's hand.

"Thank you, sir," responded the StarCraft Captain as he unconsciously wiped his hand on the leg of his officer's uniform, "but I prefer not to dwell on past successes."

Berishu was careful to avoid saying the word 'yes', as it was well-known that Ejsaanons have an inclusive view of gender and species, and would take any clear affirmation, in any context, as complete sexual license.

The terrible smell in the air intensified as his response was translated into the specific partly-digested solids, indistinguishable from Martian waste solids vapour, which the Ejsaanon could absorb and understand as language.

Some martianoid wiseacres refer to Ejsaanons as 'bags of shit'; however on their home planet, Ejsaan, that appellation is often used affectionately in connection with especially eloquent orators.

"Understood," said the translator box as Trook unconsciously wiped her shaken tentacle on one of the lower tentacle sleeves of her Commodore's uniform, as she didn't really fancy this biped. Still, she continued to flirt simply by habit. "Would you prefer then, to dwell on future successes, instead?"

"Well, um, I do prefer to dwell on future successes... or even the matters at hand. Specifically, my crew's new orders." The Captain again deftly avoided any direct affirmation.

"Excellent. I have some important news for you, Captain. The NOSFERATU has been reclassified. It is no longer a StarCraft, 2nd Class. Shall I continue?"

Overcoming his nausea to some degree by unconsciously rubbing his nose and breathing through his mouth, Berishu managed to lean forward in anticipation. This was his moment, long in the coming. All these sols stuck commanding a middling-class StarCraft, and now High Command had finally recognized him as deserving something more.

"Reclassified? As what?" asked the Captain.

"Space Corps High Command informs us that the NOSFERATU is now a, pppppl..." The translator rendered Trook's hesitation as a flatulent sound.

"Yes, I mean YESterday isn't soon enough to learn what you have to tell me..." The Captain was risking falling out of his chair. His thick eyebrows began to twitch, and his thin lips could be seen to quiver mightily beneath his tremendously fuzzy, rarely trimmed beard. (It has been speculated by some irreverent crew members of the NOSFSERATU that

9

the Captain's beard is, in actuality, a family of winter-furred Meowite forest barnacles permanently nested upon his face.)

Trook shifted uncomfortably on her resting podium. Another flatulent sound emitted but it was unclear if it was an electronic noise from the translator, or an acoustic emission from the Commodore herself.

Berishu's magic moment was going awry.

"The NOSFERATU will be serving the Alliance in a most important manner. Don't you think that is the key issue here?" asked Trwook sweetly.

"Well, service is an important value," Berishu carefully avoided any affirmation, then began to guess wildly. "Mars DefenseCraft? Extra-Galactic ExplorationCraft? Full Spectrum ScoutCraft??"

"Pppppl, incorrect, ppppppl…" The Commodore paused and watched as Berishu's hopes swelled beyond any previously charted perimeter of likelihood before continuing: "CargoShip, 3ʳᵈ Class."

"Whaa??" gasped Berishu. He felt like the air in the room had turned into quicksand.

"No need to panic, Captain. Considering your record with the Corps, we could hardly expect you to command such a reduced charge. Don't you agree?"

"Oh?" Berishu did not trust himself to deliver more than one syllable of reply.

"Indeed. You will serve as Captain on one last mission, and then…" Trook glanced at her desk screen, "Pyus Cintot, 1st class helm officer, currently aboard StarBus VI, will take command of the NOSFERATU. I trust you will not find one last voyage too degrading?"

"That will…not be a problem, sir. But what sort of a, uh, what will be my command after this mission?"

Trook averted about two thirds of her eyes. Several of her assorted orifices were seen to flex and spasm.

"At this moment, Captain, there are no suitable Captaincy openings. Pppppppl… High Command has decided that, as the best alternative to continued active service, this would be the optimal time for you to retire. Isn't that great?"

"Retire? I can't retire! I'm only twenty sols old!"

"Captain," said Trook sternly, "if High Command says you can retire, you will retire. Of course, full benefits will be extended to you. You've been with the Corps eleven sols? That entitles you to a generous fourteen and three quarter percent pension plus an eight percent discount at all Space Corps roller rinks and sugared annulus shops. Congratulations, Captain!" Trook once again overcame her distaste and offered a tentacle. "Your last mission is bound for Ksath. You have an alimental cargo, and one VIP to accompany you. Are you up for this challenge?"

Berishu ignored the offered tentacle, and the leading question. "Is Cintot a Martian?"

"Cintot is a Belaznian, for whatever difference that makes."

"Indeed, for whatever difference it makes. With your permission, sir." Berishu stood up.

"Hold on a moment, Captain. Would you like me to explain to you why you're being re-assigned?"

Berishu could see that Trook had one of her tentacles expectantly resting in a desk drawer that appeared to contain a variety of sex toys from the tri-galactic area. "I would like to know. I would like to know!" Berish repeated.

"I have nothing against Terrans, but I should say, pppppppl, that you do tend to have itchier noses than Martians, although your physiology is very similar. You want to know how that makes me feel?" Trook's far tentacle was noisily rummaging in the sex toy drawer.

"I do want to know. Tell me, please."

"It makes me feel very unlovely. When you succumb to cultural prejudice and think that my way of

11

speaking is somehow, not sexy, that hurts. Some of my best friends are Martians, and we have had the sex together."

"I find the relevance of this to my orders unclear, sir," complained Berishu.

"Captain, this is an Alliance. That means we do things together. I've come all the way from the Andromeda galaxy to ensure continued harmonious relations with Martians, and Terrans too, because we share the same values. We are all Aronists, and therefore, just like you, our dearest value is beauty. For you to ascribe its opposite to us, is far from diplomatic. We have all heard the rumours about the narrow-minded noses of Terrans, and you are a Terran."

"So I've lost my ship because I'm a Terran? That doesn't increase the beauty of the Space Corps. With all respect, sir, it doesn't contribute peace, harmony, or joy, the three cardinal elements of beauty. I mean, if we're talking Aronism, let's be clear."

"Captain, talk of Aronism from someone like yourself, a being of such limited appreciation, is quite unexpected. On Ejsaan, we all stop work for a brief period each day to mark the sunrises and sunsets so that we can appreciate the sky beauty that Aron has blessed us with. We wallow in gratitude for our daily loveliness. With you, I see no wallowing. Do you understand me, Captain?"

Berishu knew that the only thing worse than a direct affirmation with an Ejsannon, was a direct refutation.

He remained silent.

"Furthermore, these supposed unpleasant smells we communicate with actually resemble your own excrement, not ours. In that sense, you are detesting only yourselves, and your bad behaviour says more about you than about Ejsaanons. You Terrans are Martian-adjacent, and therefore should check your privilege."

"We all appreciate beauty, sir, and strive to increase it for everyone's benefit. Orders accepted!" Berishu stood, forcefully passed gas, and abruptly walked out.

The Commodore's translator decided to translate the Captain's final unexpected outburst by speaking the words: "I humbly concur."

Chapter 4. Adventures in Team Excellence

C aptain's Log 1969.031-0930   Captain Thom Berishu recording:

The NOSFERATU departed Space City C-0004 about an hour and a half ago. We are now on course for Ksath, travelling at Velocity Factor three point five. We have our cargo of 300 kilotons of Mars Bars (for the purpose of alleviating the famine), and dignitary Fis Sithis, who is to replace Tis Fithis (who was assassinated last Thursday) as the ambassador from Kduiml.

Situation nominal. Condition green.

=

Berishu slouched listlessly on his padded vinyl captain's chair. From his position he could survey all the activity around the NOSFERATU's Helm Area. The captain's chair was located at the very back of the semicircular control area; its back mere centimeters from the rear wall. The skill and paranoia of the ship's designers shone through their work.

The Captain ran his eyes over his domain left to right: the auto-lift doors; the communications console, occupied by Slaarp Cootez; the navigation console, occupied by Karp Quelfin; the helm, occupied by Ragnor Trepaloof; the science officer's console, normally occupied by Ralf, Dr. Leggentrope's replacement; and the door to the hygiene rest station, aka the little officer's room. All was quiet diligence. All was in order.

The rest station portal squeaked sharply open and discharged its occupant. Ralf, stepped lightly out, and regained his helm area position.

"Well that's it. Computer, we're out of toilet paper." said Ralf.

Berishu glanced incuriously at Ralf, then returned

his gaze to the auto-lift doors just in time to see them slide apart. With only the slightest sound of slime being squished, Fis Sithis rolled onto the Helm Area.

Sithis was Kduimlian, a native of the one sentient species considered almost as repulsive as Ejsaanons. A Kduimlian's excuse for an appendage was one droopy arm which hung out of its top, near its brain. Its body consisted of a large semi-transparent sphere, letting you see the pulsations of its various internal organs. Perhaps this was the reason most races considered Kduimlians repellent.

Kduimlians were the most impatient and insensitive of creatures. Their normal mode of transportation was hurtling themselves toward their destination like a bowling ball. Their inability to stop without assistance or collateral damage was perhaps another reason other species found them unpleasant. Sithis immediately demonstrated this by rolling over to where Berishu sat, thumping to a stop hard against the Captain's chair, leaving a sludgy mark along its side magazine pouch.

"Can I help you, Ambassador?" asked Berishu.

"Fifs. Thssp, ssth pfiff thss S," replied the slimy sphere, waving its tentacle for emphasis.

"He says 'I demand living quarters better suited to my status,'" translated Ralf who had scrambled to Berishu's side.

"It's the worst we could find," grouched the Captain.

Ralf diligently began to translate: "Ptss..."

"No! Ralf! I was kidding," Berishu interrupted, now smiling rather warmly at the Ambassador. "Tell him it's the best we have." The Captain paused for a moment, then added sotto voce, "Noranian pest." (Editor's note: Noranian meaning having to do with Nora, personification of ugliness and immortal archfoe of Aron.)

"Pssssth fifs thss SS thssp S," Ralf explained to Sithis.

"Fifst! Pppppppplllllll. Pssth fissth pssfi S. SS thss tsthp pfisthsss psssthsss ifis thssp fifs ssthsp fif fif fif fif fif sss," said Sithis.

The sentient sphere waved its tentacle in a wide circle for multiple revolutions then, with a flex of indignation, rolled away.

"What did it say?" snapped Berishu, flushing non-pastel and sweating slightly, never being able to quite get over dealing with unreasonably hostile people.

"Fine," meeked Ralf.

Other than Captain Berishu, Science Office Ralf was the only other Terran aboard the StarCraft, er, CargoShip NOSFERATU. Ralf had arrived less than a sol after his Space Corps Academy graduation ceremony on Mars, fully brain-loaded in all major Alliance languages, and reportedly ready to occupy the junior officer role. It seemed odd to Berishu that Ralf's first posting had been fully classified, with the mission file heavily redacted, despite Ralf being such a junior officer.

"Captain, may I ask a question?"

"You just did." groused the Captain. Clearly, the Academy did not ensure this young recruit had all his answers brain-loaded.

"May I ask a number of questions?"

"Such as?" For some reason, the Captain was still in affirmation-avoidance mode.

"Well, why is our helm officer asleep at his station?"

Ragnor Trepaloof was indeed asleep at his station, his face pressed into some gauzy textile he had wrapped around his hands which supported his face on the console.

"The Corps values the competence and development of our team members above all else. All helm officers are required to undergo a rigorous academic download, as well as physical training to ensure we can all rely

16

upon them in an emergency. Helm Reaction Interval is a key metric," quoted Berishu from a pamphlet he had brain-loaded long ago.

Ralf's question remained in his eyes.

"So," continued Berishu, "it is important that new helm officers are exposed to the types of stresses that occur in real emergencies, such as extended duty shifts. We can't have critical staff dozing off during a crisis. While the normal shift for an officer is twelve hours, new helm officers are required to prove they can perform a triple shift. Trepaloof is on the thirty-fifth hour of his shift."

"But that seems impossible, to stay awake for thirty-six hours," complained Ralf.

"For a martianoid that is true, and that's why I allow him to have a nap now and then. It refreshes him, and allows him to meet his triple-shift requirement at the same time," explained the Captain.

"So we have a sleeping helm officer because he is required to be awake longer than is physically possible? How does that reduce Helm Reaction Interval?"

"Once he wakes up, his HRI will be much improved. An ancillary goal is to reduce operational costs, which is one of my objectives, as Captain."

"Being an officer in the field is more complicated than they make it out to be in the Academy, I guess," admitted Ralf.

"There are some things that cannot be brain-loaded, but have to be understood in their context of competing objectives and rationalizations. That is why you are here in person. The Alliance needs more Terran officers," declared Berishu.

"They do? Why?" Ralf had been under the impression that the Alliance didn't really need very many Terran officers.

"Space Corps sees the value of all Alliance member states, and strives to ensure the Corps is fully representative of those it protects. Sure, it's mostly Martians here, but even a Terran like you or I has a chance of getting ahead." Berishu had the distinct feeling he was repeating things that he no longer believed, so he finished up with some hard-won truth. "Also, non-Martians work for less."

"So we have a sleeping helm officer because we are committed to the highest quality of helm operation achievable at the lowest possible cost?"

Berishu reached over and punched Ralf on the arm in a friendly manner.

"See? Some things you just can't brain-load!"

Chapter 5. Encounter in Space

Navigator Karp Quelfin was a Martian physically, but had been born on the planet Meow. Because of this background, he had inherited some of the traits of his home planet's people. For example, he took great joy in mathematical calculation. He also tended to lick himself a lot, as this had been strongly encouraged during his primary schooling among the feline Meowites.

This was one of the reasons he had been assigned to the position of Chief Navigator on the NOSFERATU, the math, I mean, not the licking. This was also the reason he was so competent at his job. To take it one step further, this was the reason he was the first to spot It.

"Captain!" Quelfin called excitedly. "We are on a collision course with an unidentified object!"

"Collision course?" scowled the Captain. "How long until impact?"

"Four point eight seconds, mark… now," responded Quelfin with great precision.

"Cut the engines, you fool!" bellowed the Captain.

"Not a problem," shrugged Helm Officer Trepaloof, awakened by the Captain's disturbed vocalizations, as he cut all power to the ship's enormous twin hyperdrive reactors. The bulky ex-StarCraft came to a swift halt.

"576.2 meters from the object", noted Quelfin, as he began unconsciously licking the inside of his left wrist.

The small silvery sliver which was the cause of their panic still slowly spun towards the bulky interstellar craft.

"And mark. Impact in one point seven seconds." Quelfin was determined to carry his comments of doom on until the very end.

"Shields up!" Captain Berishu ordered, with just a

hint of hysteria entering his voice.

"Too late," said Trepaloof calmly.

"Oh sweet Aron! We're all gonna die!" screamed Ralf.

The two meter long silver object struck the front section of the NOSFERATU. A terrible rending noise assaulted the ears of the crew; the ship shuddered with impact.

"Report!" The Captain waited.

"We've taken a hit in the computer section. I've sealed off the area. The damage is extensive. We have a complete loss of computers, navigation, and the electronic games in the rec. area," explained Slaarp Cootez, the Communications Officer.

"What about external communications?"

"Oh yeah. Them too," added Slaarp.

"Casualties?" groaned Berishu.

"Hmm... only ten were killed on impact. It could have been worse."

"Could have been worse??" raged the Captain. "We've only a crew of seventeen!"

"I mean we could've been killed," explained Slaarp coolly.

"True," allowed the Captain.

=

It erupted from sleep. It had lain dormant for centuries, powerless in Its nomadic coffin/prison. Since It had been captured and conquered, stopped from continuing Its bloody rampage by being sealed in a super strong container and cast among the stars, It had rested.

Now, It had been awakened. The blood-hunger again rose within It.

Soon It would kill again. Eagerly and impatiently awaiting the inevitable blood-letting, It moved restlessly about the depressurized and nearly demolished engineering section of the NOSFERATU.

=

Berishu was not expecting what happened next. His command, earlier taken away from him for obscure or possibly political reasons, now lay hopelessly damaged. The complete loss of computers and communication abilities aboard the NOSFERATU provided an existential crisis. Without computers they could not, with any accuracy, plot a course for any haven at which the NOSFERATU might be repaired. Without communications, they could not alert anyone to their predicament.

And yet, amid all these problems, Berishu found some relief: while his faithful crew had succumbed to the explosive decompression caused by the impact, so had their cargo of one slimy, annoying dignitary bound for Ksath: Fis Sithis.

Into every life, a little sun must shine, philosophized Berishu silently.

And he believed that for a moment, until the auto-lift doors slid open. Berishu's body went rigid; he screwed his eyes closed, momentarily rejecting reality. For a few seconds, only his sense of hearing was operational. Something large, round, not entirely dry, yet familiar, did roll towards him. He heard some thsspssing and some pthsssing. Now some footsteps, slow and cautious.

"Captain?" inquired Ralf timidly. Slowly Berishu unscrewed his eyes.

"Science Officer Ralf," acknowledged the Captain.

"He says he wants a baloney sandwich."

"What?" asked Berishu, but he had heard.

"Ambassador Sithis says he wants a baloney sandwich. He says crises make him hungry."

"Why isn't he dead?!" wailed the Captain.

"Uh-" Ralf's eyes flickered nervously back and forth for a moment. He directed his gaze towards Sithis, and framed Berishu's question into a polite inquiry. Soon, sibilant slurpings ensued. Ralf waited, superfluously nodding, then translated the ambassador's response.

"He was in the auto-lift car during the... incident."

While Ralf translated, the Kduimlian's one droopy appendage slimed sneakily towards the storage pouch on the side of Berishu's chair. It explored the cavity for a moment, before extracting a brown paper bag. It held the bag over its primary ingestion orifice, and turned it upside down. Two baloney sandwiches fell neatly into its gaping maw, which then closed. The bag fell, discarded, onto the floor, and the Kduimlian rolled off to bother Slaarp for a while.

"My lunch!" growled the Captain, stooping to retrieve and peer futilely inside the empty brown paper bag. "That slimy ball of slime ate my lunch!"

Doing his best to change the subject to something more pleasant, Ralf asked: "So Captain, what are you going to do to save the ship this time?"

Captain Berishu grimaced.

Chapter 6. Mostly Hapless

Berishu realized he could not devise a plan to extricate the remaining NOSFERATU personnel from the mess they were in until he knew the true extent of the damage done to his ship. Only through direct inspection could this be accomplished. The Captain therefore chose to inspect the damaged computer section personally, taking with him Science Officer Ralf and Communications Officer Slaarp Cootez.

In preparation of entering the depressurized computer section, the trio donned pressure suits. They entered the large and largely dark area cautiously, carefully weaving their way through the many pieces of debris that the impact of the mysterious object had strewn about the area.

When they finally found the rogue object, jammed against an inner bulkhead, they noted it was damaged in a very peculiar way.

The over-sized coffin was in near perfect condition, excepting a single medium-sized puncture at one end. The hole was about one square meter, and the metal on the fringe had been bent out, not in, as one might have expected.

It was as if something had broken free from inside the container.

Berishu was about to comment on this when he felt the deck suddenly vibrate beneath his feet. He whirled about.

"Behind you!" he called to the others through his suit radio.

The other two silver-clad figures spun around to face It.

The Thing was about two and a half meters tall and resembled a living, slimy tree. It had a thick vein-covered trunk which extended upwards to where it came apart in pseudo-branches. Each of those branches ended in a mouth-like orifice, lined with a ring of long and very sharp-looking, saliva-dripping, teeth.

Before the crew could further examine the fascinating creature that stood before them, It came sludging towards them.

"Re-pressurize the computer section!" Berishu radioed to the Helm Area.

The three martianoids simultaneously ran for the exit but the Thing managed to get between Ralf and the auto-lift. Slaarp Cootez, acting as the Eternal Hero, lunged in front of Ralf. The Thing extended several of its drooling branches towards the nearest officer. As the branches began to suck violently at the air around Slaarp, he felt himself drawn inexorably closer. Berishu and Ralf ran for the exit while the Thing focused its attack on Slaarp.

The suction became intense and Slaarp could resist no longer. Slowly, he was drawn towards the teeth of the Thing's main branch. There, the Thing began to chew on his head with noticeable gusto. The hapless hero's brains, mixed with blood and gore, flowed freely to the deck.

The Thing stooped to allow one long orange tongue to run over the deck, sopping up all of Slaarp's internal juices. Then It started to work on his body. First, It chewed on Its favorite parts: the arms and legs. It grinded Slaarp's bones into a delectably fine powder, and swallowed.

The Thing was in a frenzy of eating. It ripped at the already badly mangled body with Its many branches. Blood and pieces of flesh were scattered thoughtlessly around the area.

The Thing finished Slaarp off, emitted one very clearly audible belch, and that was that for the Eternal Hero.

By this time, Ralf and the Captain had made their getaway to the bulkhead doors that sealed the computer section off from the rest of the ship. Trepaloof had activated the external shields and finished re-pressurizing the area, and was therefore prepared to remotely open the bulkhead doors for the duo without delay.

The two CargoShip officers dashed past the heavy steel and styrofoam doors and down the corridor, the Thing sloshing after them. It could not slosh as fast and the Captain and Ralf could run, but still they could feel Its suction increasing. Just before the Thing-created gale became irresistible, the two officers reached the auto-lift.

In a nick of time, they were swept upwards to the Helm Area, and away from the Thing from beyond this galaxy.

Chapter 7. Brain Worms

"All right. Does everyone understand the plan?" asked the Captain.

"Yeah."

"Completely."

"Uh..."

"Ralf?"

"Well, Captain," delayed Ralf, "I don't seem to understand the part after the part where you and Karp, er, Mr. Quelfin leave the Helm Area..."

Berishu sighed.

"Ya see, Ralf," the Captain still had his patience, "Quelfin and I will be leaving the Helm Area through the auto-lift, that's the little door right over there, and going down to the Armory, picking out some suitable weapons, and hunting down the Thing. You got that okay?"

"Well, yes." Ralf hesitated. "But what do I have to do?"

"Ralf, you have the most important job of all!"

"Me?" Ralf's wide eyes told of his astonishment.

"You. You'll stay here, on the Helm Area, and, uh...." Berishu drummed his fingers together for a moment, lost in thought. "Computer, repeat Ralf's last logged input."

"Science Officer Ralf logged zero inventory for Helm Area hygiene tissue at 0932."

"Ralf," restarted the Captain. "I need you to check the hygiene tissue allocation distribution for the last resource cycle period. I want you to spot any anomalies in the usage patterns. There may be sub-optimal utilization of HT occurring in individual incidents. We need to flush out these variations to decrease the delta from our projected consumption baseline."

"Understood, Captain. I shall do my utmost in the

undertaking of this assignment," said Ralf, momentarily standing at attention, chest swelling with pride.

As Ralf turned to confront his onerous torrents of pertinent data streams, Berishu and Quelfin entered the auto-lift and left for their little chore.

=

Quelfin leaned towards the auto-lift panel and licked the 'Three' button.

"Do you have to lick everything?" asked Captain Berishu.

"It's great for my immune system," shrugged Quelfin.

The auto-lift came to an abrupt halt on Level 3. Berishu and Quelfin stepped out slowly and silently.

They discovered the area appeared clear via extensive neck craning. They also discovered that how something appears is not always necessarily how it is.

From behind them, a tremendous roar rose. The air around them started to shift. In desperation, the two officers began to run down the corridor that led to the Armory. The Thing was now in visual range, sloshing determinedly toward them.

Captain Berishu managed to escape the force of Its sucking but Quelfin, who was closer to the Thing, could not. While Berishu completed the fifty meter dash to the Armory, Quelfin barely managed to keep out of the grasp of the Thing's branches.

When the Armory doors closed behind Berishu, he muttered a long stream, or really a mid-sized river, of carefully organized obscenities. Moments later, as he sorrowfully contemplated the death of his navigator, he heard a tiny tapping at the door. Quite sure that the Thing would not tap at the door in such a restrained manner, Berishu opened the door a crack.

In the hall stood Karp Quelfin, apparently unharmed.

"Aron's belly! Karp! You're still alive!! Incredible! Sweet Tri-Galactic Esus!!" Berishu was noticeably relieved to see that his ship's complement had not been further diminished.

Quelfin stared blankly at his Captain, "Yes. So it appears." The words were spoken hollowly.

Berishu grabbed Quelfin and pulled him inside the Armory.

"What happened to It?"

"It let me go."

"What!? Why?"

"It's an old friend of my brother Seymour."

"What? You've got to be - did you get your head caught in the petawave transmitter?"

"Of course."

"C'mon, knock off the comedics."

"Then how do you expect this to sell?" asked Quelfin indignantly.

"You're not supposed to talk about that!" Berishu looked around nervously. "Now never mind," ordered the Captain. "Let's load up these weapons and get after that Thing!"

"No."

"What?" snapped Berishu, feeling like he was repeating himself.

"Seymour will get mad at us."

"Is there something wrong with you?"

Berishu was swiftly catching on, but the only reply he got came in the form of a rapid punch to the jaw. He was unconscious as he hit the floor.

Chapter 8. If You Can't Lick Them, Mutiny

When Berishu woke, Quelfin was gone. The Captain hastily scooped up a vaser pistol, plus a handful of grenades, then ran out into and down the corridor.

He made the auto-lift in record time, well not quite record time. If he had shaved just a tenth of a second off his time, then it would have been record time. Oh well, life is too short for regrets. The auto-lift car zipped upwards towards the Helm Area... if he hadn't grabbed the grenades, he probably would have had the record time, you know. Or if he had taken the grenades, but not the vaser. Or if he had left them both. Then his record would have been safe for quite some time. No one could have touched it! If he had left the vaser plus left the, uh- sorry. The auto-lift car zipped upwards towards the Helm Area.

Berishu was not expecting the reception he received. As the auto-lift doors opened, Trepaloof grabbed him and pinned him to the deck, chuckling evilly all the while.

"Heh heh. We got the nut."

"What are you doing?" screamed Berishu. "Get off me Trep! That's an order!"

"We don't take orders from you anymore, banana brains," said Trepaloof nastily.

"Pardon?" Berishu's voice was encroaching on a frequency formerly limited to the female of his species.

"They take orders from me now." Quelfin revealed his presence behind the Captain. "I told them how you attacked me just as I was about to finish off the Thing! They know that you've lost your mind," drooled Quelfin. His eyes bulged, then he licked the backs of both his hands in quick succession.

Suddenly, a flash of insight so subtle yet overt struck Berishu. In that instant, he could perceive the situation with such a clear-minded understanding that he astounded himself. Trepaloof's grenade launcher held haughtily by his side, Quelfin's insane grin (grimace?), the Kduimlian's nervous, near hyperactive, rolling back and forth, back and forth, forth and back… Something was wrong. All the minuscule hints gave the seasoned StarCraft, er, CargoShip Captain all the evidence he needed to draw to that one horrifying, yet inescapable, conclusion: something was very definitely wrong.

"Me? Lost my mind?" Berishu searched the room for a sympathetic face. "It's Quelfin who's lost his mind! He attacked me in the Armory before we even had the chance to fight that Thing!"

"Nonsense," said Quelfin with great calm, as the digestive worms from the Thing burrowed further into his brain, releasing pleasing neuro-toxins. Quelfin's eyes remained steady on Berishu, but his normally inexpressive face was contorted and glimmering with a strange inner light. He petulantly pushed a lock of shaggy, grease-shiny hair from his eyes. "Do you deny you said the Thing was an old friend of your brother Seymour?"

"What are you talking about? That's what you said!" countered Berishu.

"Poppycock," stated Quelfin. "I don't have a brother named Seymour."

"An ugly lie!" argued Berishu.

"My orders are, as of this moment, you are confined to your quarters until further notice," commanded Quelfin.

"He's gone stark raving mad!" Berishu pleaded to the others.

"Pssssssssssfif thsssif S sssssp fifsssfif. Fsthfis ssths fifs thss sspths SS! S pssfisssth. Fif fif fif fif fif fif fif fif fif fif!" spewed Sithis with great shudders of quasi-spittle-accompanied laughter.

"What did he say, in precis?" Berishu asked a grave-looking Ralf.

"He declines to agree with you."

"Shut up!" screamed Quelfin. He could tolerate the highly stylized jargon of the engineering section, but the intellectual banter of the two high-ranking officers was too much for him. "Take our mad Captain away, Mr. Trepaloof," commanded Quelfin.

"Yes, Lord of Masters," said Trepaloof using the new salute: he stuck his thumb up the appropriate nostril (his own) and wiggled the rest of his fingers.

With this formality complete, Trepaloof began to push the Captain, forcing him in small protesting steps toward the auto-lift. As they crossed the lift threshold, Ralf leapt forward and displaying some arcane militant Terran dental yogic art, grabbed Trepaloof by the furthest back, left molar and flung the disloyal crewman out the auto-lift car. The doors snapped shut behind Ralf, and the auto-lift propelled the Captain and him away from the Helm Area.

"Ralf, thank you!" the Captain cried exultantly. "Why'd you do that, save me like that?"

"It just seemed the beauty way to go. I mean, I knew he was lying, and you were telling the truth."

"But how?"

"Actually Captain, it was partly a little thing called prosody, which could technically be defined as that particular component of communication or language not directly inferred from its semantic content. An example could be like the tone of voice, or a pheromone emission. My expertise is very strong. For virtually any language, I can interpret prosody along with the more mundane and tangible-"

"So your science degree is in language?" interrupted the Captain.

"Well, no, it's a one sol apprenticeship plus qualification exam."

"For the degree?"

"For the certificate."

"You're a science officer with a certificate???"

"Well my dad was a Senator…"

"Okay, that makes sense then. So what really tipped off you that I was the sane one, and not Quelfin?"

"Actually, it was the bit about the brother named Seymour. You see, I'm the only one on this ship with a brother named Seymour. And (choke) he's no longer with us."

"No? I'm sorry about that, Ralf. What happened to him?"

"He became lost while hiking on Protein World 3, then later (sniff) was eaten by an unregistered order of Burgerbeasts.

"How terrible. Terrible and ironic."

"Yeah."

Chapter 9. Chased and Chastened

"He got away!" yelled Quelfin. "Get after them, you fools!"

Trepaloof and Sithis ran and rolled to the auto-lift. Their car zipped through Level 2. The other car zipped through Level 2. Their car zipped through Level 3. The other car zipped through Level 3. Their car zipped through Level 4. The other car zipped to Level 1.

"Somehow, they've managed to lose us," snarled Trepaloof.

"Fifisthp," sprayed Sithis obscenely.

=

Berishu and Ralf's auto-lift car was, once more, parked at the Helm Area. The doors snapped open and Berishu, glaring malevolently, stepped out.

"Gee... hi fellas. You, uh, need anything licked?" grinned Quelfin, alone and now suddenly committed to a less rigorous approach to mutiny.

Berishu began extracting Quelfin's teeth, one at a time, through his nose.

=

On Level 4, Trepaloof and Sithis exited their auto-lift car. Not knowing where to begin the search for the two traitors, a starting point was chosen at random. They headed down the corridor to their left.

=

"YYYYYAAAAAAAAAARRRRRRRRGGG!" yarged Quelfin as Berishu began to work on removing his right bottom incisor.

=

Trepaloof and Sithis arrived at the Recreation Area, entered cautiously, and found the Thing playing Solitaire. Seeing them, It began Its now familiar air sucking, causing Sithis to roll helplessly towards It.

As Its main branch grasped the living sphere and its

shining teeth burrowed into the soft flesh of the Kduimlian like so many daggers, Trepaloof raised his grenade launcher. He aimed carefully at the Thing and pulled the trigger. The launcher exploded in his hands.

At this point it might be germane to explain that it is not a smart idea to have your weapons calibrated and commissioned by the Snuggly Bunnies of Galactic Unemployment Area 7. Because even if you do save a lot of money, the Bunnies generally bungle the work.

It is furthermore not a smart idea to have your critical military materiel shipped back to you by Treadex, the intergalactic budget couriers whose jingle goes something like: if you're not in a hurry, and don't really worry, but need to save some bucks, then ship with us, that's the crux!

The force of the explosion ripped Trepaloof's body apart, and sent the Thing and Sithis sprawling. Sithis recovered first, bleeding but mobile, and swiftly rolled out of the Recreation Area.

The Thing, recovering second, squished upright and began to slosh after the gooey sphere.

Trepaloof would not be recovering third, or at all, for that matter.

"S thss fifssS tpsst fifsith thssp, SSS," prayed Sithis as he rolled toward the auto-lift in panic. He gained control of the auto-lift with the Thing less than two meters behind.

"Fsthss psp," said Sithis; he had informed the auto-life voice control that he wished to be taken to the Helm Area.

Chapter 10. Things Get as Hairy as a Zin Armpit

C *aptain's Log 1969.031-2330   Captain Thom Berishu recording:*

The NOSFERATU will pass within 336 megameters of the moon Jyuti, which orbits the colony planet Nerais, at precisely 1969.031-2335. We are therefore approximately one-fourth of the way to our destination, Ksath.

Crew Status: Twelve of the crew died upon impact of an unknown alien object at 1969.031-1047. Crew members Karp Quelfin, Ragnor Trepaloof, plus Ambassador Fis Sithis are to be charged with the following: mutiny, insubordination, assault and battery, illegal use of weapons on a (pause) CargoShip, and conspiracy. Communications Officer Slaarp Cootez died performing above and beyond the call of duty. Recommendations: Tri-leaf Cluster Award.

Condition: sickly yellow.

=

As Berishu looked up from the recording machine, the auto-lift doors whooshed open and Fis Sithis rolled limply in.

Quelfin lay semiconscious (about as lucid as usual) on the deck. He was making funny noises, trying to learn to talk without teeth.

"FffffffffffffffffssssssssssssssSSSSSSSSSfffFFFFF," said Quelfin through his gums.

"Psssssfif ssp SS, S psssssfifs fsspss ssthssp sss fifs thpsstip," said Sithis, politely replying to Quelfin's remark.

Ralf snickered.

"So you decided I'm not the crazy one after all. Eh, Sithis?" asked Berishu, obviously misinterpreting the

Kduimlian's return.

"S ssssssthssifp fif fif fif fif fif fif fif! S thss SS thstith! Fif fif fif fif fif!" Sithis smugly replied as he revealed a small vaser weapon and aimed it at Berishu.

"He says, 'you can-'," Ralf began to translate.

"I think I can figure this one out myself, Ralf," muttered Berishu.

Sithis motioned them both away from their control stations. His tentacle wavered not a millimeter. The chronometer built into the Captain's chair clicked to 2335 and through the forward viewscreen the pale blue moon Jyuti began to peek. Soon the Helm Area was illuminated by the moon's colourful emanations.

"Oh oh," said Captain Berishu as he began to sprout additional hair.

"What's the matter, Captain?" asked Ralf earnestly.

"It's the moon! Get out before it's too late!" The Captain was rapidly transforming into a giant ball of fuzz. In astonishment, the Kduimlian retreated a roll and a half.

"It's all right," Ralf confabulated. "He's just turning into a giant Snuggly Bunny. You'll see, it'll be okay. He'll be round, like you, and hairy, and he'll purr a lot, and be real friendly. His employability and productivity might be somewhat compromised, but no real problems here, no not at all..."

About this time, the Captain's mocha brown skin had erupted with a thick mat of oddly silverish brown hair. His teeth were now surmounting his lips, expanding into giant, gleaming fangs.

"I didn't know Snuggly Bunnies had fangs..." Ralf was confused.

As Berishu's eyes became wild and crazed, Sithis rolled and Ralf ran toward the auto-lift. Ralf made it; Sithis didn't. The voracious werewolf commenced ripping at the wound the Thing had earlier started on the Kduimlian. He was more successful. Soon all that was left of the Ambassador Fis Sithis was about a half kilogram of cartilage. The werewolf burped obstreperously.

Chapter 11. Survivors

After his narrow escape from the jaws of death (quite literally in this case), Ralf had taken the auto-lift to Level 3 where he hoped he would not bump into the Thing. As he stood in the corridor, he was relieved to find it empty and free of signs of conflict.

Ralf stood very still for a moment to audibly gauge his surroundings. His ears could discern nothing but a faint rasping noise. This noise did not resemble the roaring of the Thing. It also did not resemble any other noise he had previously heard. Ralf moved down the corridor to his right, towards the front part of the ship where the command and living facilities were provided. Level 3 contained living quarters only.

The horrible rasping noise grew to an anguished grating in Ralf's ears. As he rounded a corner, an open portal loomed before him. The disturbance had reached such a volume that Ralf was sure it originated from just beyond the opening. Ralf craned his neck around the edge of the doorway to peer into the room.

The terrible rasping noise continued to pound at Ralf's tympanic membrane. Spellbound, he unconsciously took a step into the room, only to discover the source of the eerie din.

Beneath the sheets on one of the beds in the room lay a huge scarlet creature. The horrible bleatings continued as Ralf slowly circled the bloated martianoid. A quivering rose and swelled within Ralf. He was now in front of the creature, at its feet. He looked down, and screamed.

A distorted Martian face rested at the far side of the bed: mouth gaping, eyes now open, staring, but unfocused. Ralf screamed again, and fell backwards into the awaiting grasp of...

=

While the frenzied werewolf was eating the Kduimlian Ambassador, Karp Quelfin managed to drag himself through the auto-lift doors. The werewolf, noting this, dropped the half-chewed remains of the alien dignitary and gave chase. But Quelfin was already gone. Slight dents appeared on the auto-lift doors as the werewolf hammered its furry paws against them in frustration. It howled in a very un-Captain-like manner.

=

Ralf's eyes were clamped tightly shut. He screamed, and screamed again, until all the terror within him had been expressed. An awesome silence followed Ralf's shrieks. The terrible roaring/rasping noise had abated. From that awful audible void, a voice issued.

"Hey buddy, you okay?"

The voice calmed Ralf somewhat, and he slowly opened his eyes. Standing in a semi-circle around him were three beings. One was an android, one was a tall male Martian, handsome enough to be a model, and the other was the scarlet creature, which looked less terrifying now.

The distorted red martianoid face was connected to a fairly normal, albeit largish, martianoid body. Ralf now peered into that face, the face of an alcoholic, or actually an alcoholic with a severe hangover. Naturally, it could be assumed that this entity was a crew member.

"Sweet Aron," the red being said. "Am I glad you quit yer bellowing. I got quite the splitting headache."

And with that comment, the red one drew a small container from one of his many bulging pockets, unscrewed the lid of said container, and began to ingest more of another favorite intoxicant. The name tag on his baggily pocketed pants read 'Snorg Ballesto - Technician'.

The 'droid's tag read 'Anark 337', and the third survivor, the handsome male's, read 'Swep Fetherhed - Helm Officer (3rd Class)'.

Ralf gave the three a careful once-over. The first to go under Ralf's scrutiny was Snorg Ballesto.

Snorg was not as non-martianoid as Ralf had first believed. He was just your basic martianoid slob. He appeared to be in his late twenties, clearly middle-aged. What little hair the man still had was long and carefully combed over so as to cover his many bald patches. He wore a pair of faded and creased work pants, along with an off-white t-shirt. To the left of his navel was a small hole in the shirt. Somehow this emphasized his rotund belly.

Being that Snorg was an Ihnewian, he tried his best to rarely blink. You'll understand later.

Beneath his stringy hair there lay a face that, to say the least, was ruddy. Huge scarlet ears hung on the sides of his head.

Ralf's first impressions of Snorg were not limited to what he could see. As he gazed upon this crew member, he could still hear the deeply strained sound of breathing. One thing: Snorg would be excellent at doing creepy voice-overs.

To Snorg's left, stood Swep Fetherhed. Crowning Swep's head was a fine patch of soft blonde hair, styled immaculately in accordance with the latest trends. It struck Ralf that Swep would be one of the few people aboard the NOSFERATU wearing clean, matching socks.

Ralf remembered Swep from his first day on the NOSFERATU, when it had been docked at Space City C-0007. Several new crew members had been assigned that day, and as they mingled in the loading bay with the existing crew, they were invited to a meet-n-match event aboard the Space City.

These events were often spawning grounds for short-term romance as these crew shipped out for long duration trips, often aboard ships with small complements and limited holo entertainment.

A female had approached Ralf and asked him his home province, clearly mistaking him for a Martian.

"I'm actually a Terran. From Newer York. My Dad used to be a Senator." explained Ralf.

"That's impressive. I don't usually meet a lot of Terrans. Did your Dad's third eye help him get into the Senate?" asked the Martian blonde sweetly.

"Third eye?" Ralf's forehead wrinkled. "Terrans don't have a third eye."

"Well some do, you just can't see it. It's all over HoloTime. They use it to manipulate people, financially or sexually. It's not very lovely. So, you don't have one, that's what you're saying?" she asked suspiciously.

"It's just a myth. Martians and Terrans are exactly the same. The DNA shows it," explained Ralf patiently.

"Well, the idea itself is kind of ugly, so maybe we should avoid it by having you stay away from the meet-n-match. Won't that be nice?" she asked everyone else in the room, turning away from Ralf.

"Now wait a minute," Swep said, stepping closer to the blonde. "There's no reason to exclude someone based on these kinds of scurrilous rumours. We are all Alliance, and we all add to the wonder and splendour of our beautiful civilization. Each of us is worthy of love. Ralf, let me welcome you to the team, and let me escort you to the meet-n-match personally."

"Or," the blonde had teased Swep, "You could stay aboard, and have acrobatic zero-g sex with me..."

"Sorry, Ralf." Swep had then taken the blonde's hand and led her away.

Despite this, Ralf had been impressed with Swep's potential integrity, and was now glad to see him alive.

The 'droid Anark 337 stood to Swep's other side. The grey mobile computer was a loose caricature of a Martian male. Interestingly enough, the synthetic fibers on Anark's head were styled in a manner much like

Swep's. Anark series 'droids are been known to imitate persons they understood to be of high social status. Apparently Anark 337 was doing his best to imitate the suave Swep.

Ralf did not see this as an attempt on the 'droid's part to better itself, but as another example of the conformity of the beings who made up the Alliance. If there's one thing I can't stand, thought Ralf, it's people without a little individuality, a little flamboyance. He then reached down and retied his grey-toned no-name sneakers.

=

Quelfin exited the auto-lift at Level 3. He turned left to enter the Armoury. Once inside, he began stuffing his pockets with grenades. Also, he obtained a small vaser pistol, and an automatic disperser rifle. The brain worms hate it when their host runs out of ammo.

=

On the other side of Level 3, Ralf and his new-found allies were making plans.

"Well, the entire computer complex, except for the automatic functions, all wiped out," admitted Ralf. "We've no automatic navigation, no automatic food processing, no electronic Whack-A-Mole. This is gonna be tough."

"I believe I have a plan," Anark 337 stated flatly. "Do we still have communication ability?"

"Just internal," gloomed Ralf.

"What about auto-distress?"

"Well, technically, yes. Auto-distress could still be functioning, but it won't help. Our velocity is still over c, so we can't transmit with the low gain antenna anyway," explained Snorg.

"In the event we exit hyperspace, there is a moderate chance of rescue before the ship life support system fails. The ship is now just past the Nerais system, so that means the next system along our vector... (Anark paused to retrieve some secondary memory information) Betrsoe. Minimum range at 1969.032-0930 which is approximately one hour from now."

Anark's careful planning was interrupted by a loud thumping and roaring. Pieces of metal and plastic flew as the Thing burst through the door and into the room.

"I will remedy the situation through all viable means!!" stated the maintenance 'droid at maximum volume.

Anark promptly jumped in front of the killer alien. Three of the Thing's branches reached out and grappled the brave machine. Sparks and pieces of syntha-flesh flew. The 'droid was being ripped apart.

Realizing It had been cheated of the organic food in the room, the Thing flung aside the pieces of 'droid and started to slosh after Ralf, Swep, and Snorg. But they were already through the door, and running down the corridor.

About halfway to the auto-lift, Snorg tripped on one of the grenades that Captain Berishu had dropped earlier. The small bomb exploded and pieces of Snorg littered the corridor. A vague odor of barley hung in the air.

The Thing, temporarily slowed by this brilliant tactic, could not prevent Ralf and Swep from reaching the auto-lift.

"Where to?" Ralf asked Swep.

"Level 1, the Helm Area."

The car stopped at the terminal on the top level of the NOSFERATU. The two haggard heroes hopped out. The Helm Area was splattered with bits of Kduimlian carcass, but otherwise deserted.

Chapter 12. Glint Power

When Quelfin had finished loading up with weapons, he left the Armoury with a new purpose in life. He had to save the NOSFERATU by assassinating the insane officer who would lead her to ruin, an officer named Thom Berishu.

The digestive worms that the Thing had initially infected him with now began to burrow deeper into his brain stem, triggering further paranoid delusions.

=

The Captain was exhausted. He had spent most of nine hours ripping apart various sections of the NOSFERATU.

"You destroy the thing you love most," quoted Berishu approximately.

But his rampage was over. They had finally passed the moon Jyuti and he had returned to his martianoid form. Now he lay on the deck of the aft section of Level 2.

Several grenades that he had earlier placed in his belt were missing. He wondered where they were. He doubted if he, in his werewolf form, would use grenades. He didn't recall using any grenades, but then again, he didn't recall not using any. Feeling in his pocket, he discovered that his vaser pistol was also missing. He sat upright, and began to collect his wits.

=

"What we do is: we drop the ship out of hyperspace. Then the auto-distress can heard by Betrsoe, I mean, if the low gain antenna is actually working. Also, if we can, we alter our course so we travel closer to the inner planets, that would improve our chance of being noticed," explained Swep, moving his hands through the air in a way that inspired confidence in his audience.

"Furthermore, and crucially, if we add a rotational element to our motion, the cylindrical configuration of our craft will produce a characteristic vadar plot that will distinguish us from natural phenomenon."

Seeing Ralf not reacting to his explanation, Swep continued. "If we spin, we produce a glint, a wink to the cosmos! They will see the flash of our hull. This technique was used long ago, to look for spent rocket boosters, way back in pre-antigrav days. That should get us some attention." Swep smiled and winked, with one of his prominently bright front teeth sparkling with charisma, and almost blinding the star-struck Ralf.

"How much attention?" Ralf managed to ask, peering past the glare of Swep's dental brilliance.

"Well, not as much as a guest slot on Real Snouts Live, that holo-oinkfest of pink cuteness!" joked Swep.

Perhaps this is what it takes to lead, thought Ralf. To reflect and dazzle, add some spin, get some attention, and provide a glint.

"That sounds great, but..." began Ralf, shaking his head to painfully re-ground himself back into the ugly reality facing them. "You're just a Third Class Helm Officer. Are you sure you can do any of those things? I mean, with the shape the ship is in now..."

"But we've got to!" Swep said forcefully, finally snapping, and jamming his fingers up into his perfect hair, with some superbly manicured Orbital Black (Space Corps Official Colour #FFFF) fingernails peaking through. "Don't you see? It's the only chance, for you, for me, for all of us!!"

"Look Swep, knock off the dramatics. This ain't no B movie," admonished Ralf.

Swep relaxed, and grinned a cynic's half-mouth grin. "Not yet."

=

Berishu managed to hoist himself to a standing position. He let out a grunt for his efforts, then slowly

45

started down the corridor toward the auto-lift.

At that moment, Karp Quelfin leapt out of the auto-lift shout/spraying "You've had it now, coconut cerebrum!"

Apparently his mastery of verbalization had recovered, but his ability to restrain his saliva had not.

Quelfin fired a barrage from his disperser. Grabbing one of the grenades from his belt, he ripped out the pin and hurled the formidable little silver sphere toward Berishu.

The Captain dodged the disperser fire, caught the grenade in one hand, and threw it back to Quelfin. The explosion disintegrated the auto-lift terminal and a large part of the nearby deck between Levels 2 and 3. Quelfin had escaped serious injury by stepping behind a bulkhead.

Berishu then implemented his escape. His feet pounded the way to the next auto-lift terminal before the dust kicked up by the explosion could be settled by the fire suppression system.

Chapter 13. There's No Substitute for Expertise

When the Captain's auto-lift car arrived at the terminal by the Helm Area, Ralf and Swep were trying to figure out how to change the ship's course. Ralf was the first to notice Berishu's shaky entry.

"Captain!"

"Ralf."

"I trust we shall not encounter any more moons on our way to Ksath?"

"No." Berishu smiled weakly. "There was just one."

"What's all this about moons?" Swep asked either of the two.

"Nothing, a private joke," shrugged Ralf. "Uh, Captain? Would you be so kind as to disengage the hyperdrive reactors for us?"

"Certainly," said Berishu as he stepped over to the console and flipped the switch marked 'HYPDRV Reactors: On/Off' to the Off position.

The NOSFERATU fell out of hyperspace.

=

Captain's Log 1969.032-0900   Captain Thom Berishu recording:
We will be within communication range of Betrsoe in approximately one half hour. To add to the list of charges to be filed against Chief Navigator Karp Quelfin: treason, mutiny, insubordination, attempted murder, vandalism, disturbing the peace, assaulting a fellow officer, destroying public property, destroying private property, littering, loitering, and improperly completing a Form 401-b, "Application for Travel Expense Reimbursement".
Crew Status: It is now known that Swep Fetherhed and Snorg Ballesto did not die at the time of the impact of the alien object. Since then, Snorg Ballesto has died during the performance of his duties. Also dead is

Ragnor Trepaloof. Missing are Kduimlian Ambassador Fis Sithis and Karp Quelfin. It is not assumed that Quelfin is dead. Being that this ship cannot be run with a crew of less than four, the remaining crew (T. Berishu, S. Fetherhed, Ralf) will attempt to change the ship's course to somewhere in the inner Betrsoe system. Without the aid of computer, and with minimal power, we have little hope of rendezvousing with hypothetical rescue ships.

Condition: void black.

=

"We need someone to switch the power for helm control from the Emergency Helm Area back to the Helm Area," stated Swep.

"Someone's got to go down there, huh..." reasoned Berishu.

"That's right. We need to regain control over the ship. Somebody has got to go and switch that power back to where it belongs," stated Science Officer Ralf in a brash voice, the adrenaline bursts of the day finally getting to him.

"Absolutely right, Ralf. Two of us should do the deed." It was plain Berishu agreed wholeheartedly with Ralf.

"Two people? Er, who did you have in mind Captain?" Ralf suddenly regretted his earlier brashness. Now he remembered why he usually avoided such firm stances on subjects.

"Gosh, I don't know, Ralf. I guess I'll just have to decide after I get there." Berishu's stress had morphed into condescension. He motioned Swep into the auto-lift, and the doors slid shut behind them.

Exhausted, Ralf sat down to nervously await Berishu's decision.

=

Quelfin was about to take the auto-lift up to the top level when he realized someone was in the auto-lift shaft he planned to use. The mysterious car was heading down to Level 4. Quelfin took a car from a different terminal and pursued whomever it might be.

=

The auto-lift doors slid open. Berishu and Swep strode forth, quickly setting a severe pace for their walk to the Emergency Helm Area.

"This way. Just down the corridor," explained Berishu.

They traveled for about twelve meters before deciding to try a left turn.

"It should be around here, somewhere..." commented Berishu, again drawing on his near inexhaustible cranial reservoir of data pertaining to the NOSFERATU.

They had just started to examine the labels on some of the portals nearest them when Quelfin jumped out from behind a large abstract sculpture.

In midair, Quelfin yelled "Watch it! He could be dangerous!"

Quelfin relieved a grenade of its firing pin, and hucked it toward the Captain. Berishu caught the grenade, and lobbed it back so it sailed over and past Quelfin's head.

As it exploded, Quelfin muttered, "I gotta quit doing that."

The blast hurled Quelfin on top of Berishu.

Hearing the detonation, the Thing came sloshing.

While Swep ducked into the Emergency Helm Area, Berishu and Quelfin began to flee down the corridor. They ran in the opposite direction of the Thing, and quite wisely so.

The Thing, in some rudimentary way, understood It could not catch the rapidly receding twosome, and so elected to stay at the Emergency Helm Area's door and do Its best to forcibly enter and eat whatever flesh was contained there.

In the Emergency Helm Area, Swep frantically searched for the proper control. The Thing beat relentlessly on the air-tight, but not indestructible, portal.

Swep found the intercom system, the fuel gauges, the Hyperdrive Reactor On/Off switch, the battle console, and the built-in cola machine. But he still could not locate the power switches.

The gate to Swep's sanctuary gave a nasty crackle, and began to bend. With a howl of triumph, the Thing renewed Its attacks.

"Aron, sweet Esus," moaned Swep. Then he spotted the power switches. A partial triumph. He leapt to them. He managed to flick two of switches into the override position before the Thing and he shared the same room. He flicked two more before the Thing reached him. He flicked a final switch, then lost the ability to concentrate on the well-being of the NOSFERATU. Somehow, imminent death serves to disturb the concentration for the task at hand of those about to die.

Several of the Thing's tentacles grasped Swep, each securing an appendage. With a savage yank, Swep became a plural quantity. Five equal parts. And thus ends the saga of Swep Fetherhed, Helm Officer 3rd Class, imported beer drinker, high school quarterback, and all-round nice guy.

Chapter 14. Beaten, but not Licked

Berishu slowed. The Thing was no longer behind him. Quelfin slowed, realizing the same. Berishu sped up, realizing Quelfin was still close behind him. Quelfin sped up, realizing the same.

"Hold it right there, Berishu." Quelfin had vaser in hand. "Stop, or I'll stop you."

Berishu stopped.

A small grin slipped out of Quelfin's mouth. It trickled onto his chin and Quelfin irritably wiped it on his sleeve. Berishu rolled his eyes in disgust.

"Don't you want to lick that up?"

"Get over here," ordered Quelfin, ignoring the question. Berishu moved towards him.

"That's far enough."

Keeping his eyes on the Captain, Quelfin leaned over to the far side of the corridor and pressed a button located there. A heavy door near the Captain slid back to reveal a tiny room with a set of flimsy plastic lockers, and another door opposite the first.

"Get in."

"You're kidding!" protested the Captain.

"I am?"

"Sure you are!"

"No, I'm not."

"Sure yar. Ha! Ha!" Berishu's bonhomie was without effect.

"What part of your body would you like me to fry first?" asked Quelfin, waving the vaser meaningfully about.

"Catch you later," sighed Berishu as he stepped into the airlock.

"Goodbye!" spat Quelfin.

The heavy airlock door slid snugly shut behind Berishu.

As he heard the door seal, Berishu immediately sprung into action. Before Quelfin could take his finger off the button which had sealed the airlock door, Berishu had already opened the before-mentioned flimsy plastic locker and withdrawn a standard issue Space Corps pressure suit. His sols of training at the Space Corps Academy were finally being put to an exigent test. When Berishu had graduated from Space Survival 101, he had been able to check, enter, and seal a standard 'suit in fractionally less than twenty seconds. That had been many sols ago.

Now, during those few brief seconds Berishu struggled with the 'suit, his mind moved at an incredible pace. He tried to concentrate on his survival, but his life seemed to be flashing before his eyes. His early sols in school: trying to attain high grades by thinking like the average token Terran. Success through conforming to the dominant culture's prejudices. His thesis at the Academy, which had simply paraphrased a few other papers that implied Terrans as terrible people who require Martian guidance on an economic, political, social and personal basis, provided a B+, and a sufficient sop to Martian biases so that Berishu could be considered 'one of the loyal ones'.

After long sols of above-average work and several delayed promotions, he finally landed his much desired position as StarCraft Captain.

Berishu looked back on his life and regretted every 'aye, sir' and praise for a superior's mediocre idea while a radically brilliant one lay stifled in his own head. This was the price to be paid for success. Space Corps was no place for a thinking Terran, and that was too bad, Berishu finally realized.

Twelve seconds had passed.

Quelfin let another small grin slip out of his mouth. He didn't bother to wipe this one away. Instead, he reached for another small button near the airlock door.

He muttered "So long, mango medulla," and pressed the button.

Berishu estimated that approximately sixteen seconds had passed since the door had sealed behind him. He had both his legs and arms in the 'suit. All that remained for him to do was place the helmet over his head and seal it. He was not overly optimistic about his chances.

Then he felt a tremendous movement of air, and the coldness of the void touched him.

Quelfin was pleased. He laughed, and he laughed hard and long and loud. In fact, he laughed so hard and long and loud that the Thing decided to stop over his way to see what the big joke was.

Quelfin continued laughing right up until he realized it was time to scream.

Chapter 15. Fahrenheit 2451

S itting in front of the Helm Area's communication console, Ralf remotely watched Swep enter the Emergency Helm Area, Then he watched the Thing enter the Emergency Helm Area. Ralf watched as power came back to the Helm's computer banks.

As Berishu entered the airlock, Ralf gaped at the console screen, then turned away, unable to watch the Captain's final moments.

When the Thing and Quelfin had their final confrontation, Ralf watched and experienced some sort of mild satisfaction, along with some nausea.

Now Ralf was totally alone. He was on a deserted spaceship, with minimal computer operation. There was no one to help him. For what it was worth, aboard the CargoShip NOSFERATU, Ralf was in command.

=

Captain's Log 1969.032-0930   Science Officer Ralf recording:
Swep managed to return partial power to the helm and computers. I am not brain-loaded extensively in spacecraft navigation, so I have plotted the only course of which I am able. The NOSFERATU is now aimed at the center of the star Betrsoe. In eighteen hours, this ship will cease to be. Within nine point five hours, the temperature aboard the NOSFERATU will be too great for life to remain. I have no way of knowing if the auto-distress is transmitting. I hope so, otherwise I'm going to have a very close view of Betrsoe.
Crew Status: Captain Thom Berishu is missing and assumed dead. Recommendation: Tri-leaf Cluster Award. Also, Karp Quelfin is dead. Recommendation: Nobody send flowers.
The unclassified being that came aboard with the alien object is assumed dead, as shortly after all other life

aboard this ship had been extinguished, I depressurized
the entire ship, with the exception of the Helm Area.
Condition: warm orange.

=

*Captains's Log 1969.032-1200   Science Officer Ralf
recording:*
The interior temperature is now 309 degrees Kelvyn. If
I am not rescued by 1900 hours I will be dead. This
computation is 'on the outside.' At the earliest I could
easily die of heat exhaustion by 1400.
Crew Status: Helm Officer Swep Fetherhed was killed
performing above and beyond the call of duty.
Recommendations: Annai-Gamma Decoration.
Condition: toasty red.

=

*Captain's Log 1969.032-1653   Science Officer Ralf
recording:*
The… interior temperature in… is now (pause) …uh…
318… now 319. I'm not sure… where… uh… sweet
Jammy Handtrickes… when the… (pause)
Condition: unconscious.

Book 2. Strange in a Stranger Land

It is a tale
Told by a Terran
Full of product placements
and cross-promotion
Not necessarily historical
But truthful

- from "The Newest Of All"
by Jammy Handtrickes

[3rd Album of Aron
<Vinyl Source A404>]

Dramatis Personae

Adept (Terran)   **He certainly is**

Agmewobbialluyllsesmeecolysion   Father, Ralf's

Menni Deeh (Zin)   Science Officer, GARGOYLE

Ginus (Fenianian)   Village sage, Mont

Myelin Jaylo (Delaroug)   Ensign, STARSLAMMER

Jrrak   **Great God of Tssarofentiasterogliss**

Elder Lowm (Fenianian)
          Tribal elder, Forest of 1003 Names

Mick (Belaznian)
          Owner/operator, THREE DAY WEEKEND

Dewlod Pretze (Zin)   Helm Officer, GARGOYLE

Rip (Fenianian)   Native, Forest of 1003 Names

Siso Sbor (Belaznian)   Captain, STARSLAMMER

Halfnose Swash (Zin)   First Mate, GARGOYLE

Gwer Weyn (Zin)   Captain, GARGOYLE

Chapter 1. The Sheriff

Space Patrol Report 1969.037-0900 Captain Siso Sbor recording:
The CargoShip NOSFERATU was reported to have disintegrated as it neared the star Betrsoe at approximately 1969.032-1822. This information comes from an Alliance observatory on Tilynal (Betrsoe). The cause for this incident is not known (pause)

"Myelin, get me a list of the officers that were aboard the NOSFERATU," ordered Captain Siso Sbor of her subordinate, the Ensign Myelin Jaylo.

"Yes'm."

Myelin asked the Space Patrol Scout STARSLAMMER's computer the appropriate question, and soon drew one small data pod from a slot located near her lower left appendage. After a quick glance to verify it was the correct list, Myelin passed it to her Captain.

"What's this?" fumed Sbor. "Are we using pink data pods again? Didn't we order aquatic blue? Who requisitioned this??"

The Captain turned the little pink bauble over and over in her hands, before pulling it open, into its rectangular viewing shape.

Her question was somewhat rhetorical as Sbor and Myelin were the only crew stationed aboard the STARSLAMMER.

"Actually..." began the roughly cylindrical mass of bubbly pink stuff seated at the navigation controls.

Sbor glanced sharply at her Ensign.

"Yes?"

"I ordered it. I think it's a nice colour! What's wrong with pink!?" babbled the pink cylinder, a smudge of ruddiness creeping onto the ventral surface of her eye stalks.

"Okay, okay." Sbor sighed. "So maybe it's not so bad. It's just not the type of thing you'd expect. Usually we order the basic white pods for the computer or, you know, aquatic blue might be a nice change..."

"Nobody likes pink," groaned the cylinder. Then, more angrily, "Typical, typical!"

"This is no cause for an emotional outburst," warned Sbor. "You'll watch your attitude while you're serving on my ship, Ensign. After all, you didn't get where you are by acting like this!" preached the Captain.

"Was it my fault I couldn't afford an education?" mumbled Myelin.

"Let's hear no more whining. I just won't tolerate it. Do I make myself clear?" continued the Captain.

"Abundantly clear." The pink cylinder smirked inwardly, silently tickled at the thought of her Captain turning transparent with sexual longing as the biology of her species, the Delaroug, dictated. She pictured her Captain licking the male tuber of an aged, crimson Delaroug who remained less than transparent even when fully aroused due to a lifetime of very poor hygiene.

=

Siso Sbor was, as Berishu had been, a citizen with ambitions. While Berishu had sought to rise through the ranks of Space Corps, that intergovernmental force that dealt with defence and official relationships between the numerous governments that comprised the Alliance, Sbor rose through the ranks of Space Patrol, the basic law enforcement and traffic controllers of inter-galactic transit.

Sbor realized that to rise into the upper ranks of Space Patrol she must not only perform efficiently, but prove herself exceptional. She wholeheartedly approved of this system. Sbor was not ambitious merely because she was a careerist. She did not see her position as just a job, or a compensation profile; she was a firm believer in the sacredness of the Alliance's laws. These were her life's constants.

Once she had been told that all laws were arbitrary, designed to fit their specific society's needs, not constants, not universal. She had slapped this person. Twice. Then grabbed him by the neck beads and drawn his face close to hers. She had spoken in quiet but powerful tones to him, and released him. There now exists a Martian university graduate student who is actively searching for a definition of the phrase 'pinko commie'.

The Captain touched the 'pause' button on her log machine.

(unpause) Please see the attached list of Space Corps Officers now presumed dead. A later entry will outline possible civilian losses. End report.

With thoughts of later reports and possible later promotions dancing in her mind like the visions of sugarbugs that dance through the minds of Martian youth on Tri-Galactic Esus Giving Day, Captain Sbor leaned back in her captain's chair, savouring the moment of calm, and letting her Ensign tend to the functioning of the Space Patrol Scout STARSLAMMER.

Chapter 2. When the Star Kings Lie

Ralf lay on a soft surface. He could hear only two things: the subdued beeping and blipping of a computer, and a gentle hiss he guessed to be a ventilation system working properly.

After a few moments, another sound entered his consciousness. The sound of organism-based forced air displacement: breathing. Ralf realized someone was standing quite close, in fact, directly over him.

With only a tiny bit of effort, Ralf managed to flutter his eyelids. The light made his eyes water, but with a few more blinks, things became quite clear.

A large martianoid stood over him. It breathed again, more of a sigh this time. The martianoid possessed a full head of shaggy and matted black hair. The face was creased, and dark. A moustache and barbiche distracted from the scarred and asymmetric lips. Was it Berishu, alive but disfigured in some horrific accident?

Ralf struggled against the restraints to twist his head and gain a view of the entire chamber. One wall was computer banks, while the other contained three doors. He faced a blank wall, and could not see what was behind him. Despite limited data, Ralf came to a concrete conclusion: he was aboard a Zin pirate spacecraft.

The situation was clearly not beautiful.

The Zin lived only for material gain, being a race of plunderers, killers, and heartless spaceball card traders. No other race known to the Alliance, or even the Friggian Federation (the prime enemies of the Alliance) were as cruel.

The Zin pirate smiled, revealing a few badly yellowed teeth and much darkness, and Ralf's memory of him returned.

"Well, if it ain't my old bombing buddy Wino Weyn," grinned Ralf, the muscles in his neck taut against the bed's restraints. One summer, two sols earlier, when Ralf was between sols at private school, he had applied as a wine steward aboard an interstellar ship, his first off-planet job.

Ralf had not realized the position was on a Zin pirate vessel, and barely managed to escape lifelong service by claiming olfactory injury due to an incident with a faulty cork on a pressurized container of Centauri mold peppers.

In his quarter-sol term with the Zin, Ralf had ingratiated himself to certain crew members, Weyn especially, and managed to escape with his life after a mutinous battle (spawned by Weyn) aboard that Zin ship.

"I prefer just Weyn. I'm onan now," twitched the smile of Captain Gwer Weyn. Onan was Zin pirate slang for commanding one's own ship.

"Wow. That's a surprise. I never thought you'd manage to get a berth on a Zin ship, any Zin ship, after that Terra liner incident-"

"Hang on there. That stuff is totally inadmissible," Weyn's eyes darted nervously about him, forever on the watch for assassins.

"How is it inadmissible?" Curiosity got the better of Ralf.

"It inadmissible because I would never admit it!" roared a grinning Weyn.

"Well, thank you, Weyn. I just about burned up on the NOSFERATU. Thanks for saving my life."

"You're okay, Ralf, even if you aren't a Zin. You saved my life once, so I choose that you live now."

Ralf grinned at Weyn. Ralf grinned at the room. Ralf grinned in gratitude. What else could he do? Ralf grinned some more. There's only so long you can keep someone strapped motionless in a bed.

"You are my guest, and I don't lie," Weyn assured him, and bent to undo Ralf's restraints.

Simultaneously, a Space Patrol heavy cruiser popped out of hyperspace mere hundreds of km from the bow of the GARGOYLE. Klaxons immediately sounded inside the GARGOYLE. Several streaks of deadly light streaked out from the Space Patrol Craft and struck the GARGOYLE.

The intercom in the Zin ship's Sickbay crackled into life: "Captain Weyn to the Bridge... Captain Weyn to the Bridge..."

"Bridge?" asked Ralf.

"Yeah. We're Zin pirates. We don't care if we infringe Star Trek's copyright."

Weyn grasped Ralf by his tunic and pulled him out of the bed.

"C'mon," explained Weyn, as he dragged Ralf to the Bridge, his Bridge.

Chapter 3. Lateral-Move Career Opportunity

The Space Patrol heavy cruiser was preparing to fire again as the GARGOYLE disappeared into hyperspace. Moments earlier, Captain Weyn had gained the Bridge and commanded, "Into hyperspace!"

As the GARGOYLE entered hyperspace, the usual loud POP resounded through the ship.

"Geez, I hate that!" whined Weyn's Science Officer, Menni Deeh.

Weyn shot her an impatient look.

"Sure is a nice ship you got here, Weyn," complimented Ralf.

"Truer words..." Gwer Wevn ran an affectionate hand over his command chair. "They don't make ships like this anymore."

Right, thought Menni, now they have safety standards. She was the newest and least favourite member of Weyn's crew. Some of the crew had already complained about her low libido.

"You just can't get a ship like this anywhere anymore!" Weyn grinned to himself. "Authentic leather command chair, real oak and teak interior..."

"Captain-" Weyn's Science Officer had spoken.

"Yes, Menni?" asked Weyn wearily.

"Er, clearly that chair is vinyl. And the interior? All plastic." Menni gave a solid piece of 'oak' a knock. A hollow sound resulted. "See?"

Captain Weyn's face twisted horribly for about a half minute. Finally, he shouted "Insubordination!", drew his vaser, and transformed Menni into a hot pile of muck.

"So, now that you're here, what are your plans?" Weyn asked Ralf.

"I-" Ralf tore his eyes from the sight of the bubbling puddle of semi-liquid matter that used to be a science officer. "I guess I might see if you have a position open on your nice, uh, really excellent ship..."

"Well, let's see." Weyn stroked his chin with the tip of his vaser. Red burnt marks appeared on his chin, and a scorched beard smell wafted out, but he did not appear to notice. Zin have the best stimulants because they use them all the time. "We seem to have a science officer position open." Weyn blinked hard, and his weapon pointed vaguely towards Ralf.

"So I see. I guess that would suit me fine." Ralf stared at the tip of the weapon, still glowing from its earlier discharge.

"Okay, you're in. I tell you, it's perfect timing I found you. I'll be needing a strong right hand for my next raid, and I don't lie." The Zin shook his weapon barrel at Ralf, as if it were his finger wagging to emphasize a point.

"You want a strong right hand, you got one!" Ralf swallowed hard and settled himself onto the science officer's chair. "Now, tell me about your next raid."

Ralf suddenly noticed, with much distaste, that he had seated himself without bothering to clear the remains of the previous science officer. Weyn, not seeing this, or possibly ignoring it, carried on.

"Through a very reliable source of mine, I've discovered the timing and route of a ship with a cargo of valuable, undetectable small arms. We plan to intercept and overpower them. My source claims it's only a small, poorly armed ship. They are counting on secrecy as a defence, rather than power." Weyn smiled blandly at the thought. He clearly saw the advantages of raw power.

"Small arms," pondered Ralf. "You shouldn't have any problem finding someone to retail those. Looks like you're in for a nice profit."

"That's my motivation," lied Weyn.

Chapter 4. How to Influence Enemies and Melt New People

"There are no flaws in the plan!" argued GARGOYLE Helm Officer Dewlod Pretze. He was facing a small group of other crew members who were also dissatisfied with Weyn's command.

"We cannot fail. If we take command when he is most vulnerable, we shall not fail!" Dewlod glared about him, searching for any eyes which resisted his purpose.

The situation was clear to all present in the crew lounge. Gwer Weyn had overstepped his rights. As a Zin Captain, he had clear prerogative to mutilate, torture, and slowly kill those he deemed incompetent. Such is the way of the Zin. But Weyn had killed crew for reasons not recognized by Zin honour: he had killed crew in emotional arguments, because of choice in music, because of Zin politics, and even for personal/sexual reasons.

Weyn had clearly overstepped himself. The time for mutiny had arrived.

It was Dewlod Pretze who had guided and advised some of the finer tactical minds on the GARGOYLE (not saying much) in devising the plan of action which would transfer Weyn's power to Dewlod. With the transfer accomplished, Dewlod would show his gratitude to his comrades by dismissing the rest of Weyn's semi-loyal crew, radically promoting those who had assisted him, and refreshing the ship's complement by drawing from the pool of loners watering in the countless bars on the planet Zin.

The plan? The mutineers would attack and kill Weyn simultaneously as the GARGOYLE attacked its prey, the THREE DAY WEEKEND. Of course, Ralf would be killed with Weyn, as he was of no use to Dewlod. What use was a non-Zin on a Zin pirate ship?

=

Ship's Log 1969.37-1330   Captain Gwer Weyn recording:

We are closing in on the THREE DAY WEEKEND. Momentarily, we will contact the crew and demand their cargo. This should be an extremely easy loot and scoot despite the fact that I've noticed the crew has been displaying an extremely bad attitude lately. There's a noticeable streak of unrest in the crew. I've had to discipline three more crew members (internal note: remember to pick out two engineers and a weapons technician next time we're at Zin) and this hasn't helped morale either. Zin pirates just don't seem to be as hardy as they used to be. Sometimes I have my serious doubts about the future of Zin.

Anyhow, I'm rambling a bit. The efficiency of the crew seems sufficient for this raid.

(pause)(unpause)

My new science officer, Ralf, is coming along fine. A couple sols ago, he saved me when he was a co-op student on my previous ship. His powers of translation helped me pick out a non-contract cellphone plan, which I have kept ever since. That custom data plan covers all my needs! Anyway, it appears Ralf has managed to adapt most of his knowledge of tri-galactic culture and Space Corps operations to suit the requirements of a Zin science officer.

=

Weyn leaned back from the keyboard he had been hunched over for the last ten minutes. He had typed the final part of his log entry into the computer rather than using the standard audio interface, as he did whenever he had an entry he wished his crew not to hear. Any admission of weakness, or of inefficiency in his crew, drove Weyn to use the keyboard. Weyn's power was his ego, and he would not allow either to be diminished.

"Are we in range yet?" asked Weyn of the helm officer on duty, Dewlod Pretze.

Dewlod stared intently at a little blue screen on the helm for several long silent moments. Just as Weyn figured Dewlod would ignore his question completely, Dewlod raised his head.

"Yeah. We're in range now. Why?"

A helm officer has no right to question his captain, thought Weyn as his fingers played thoughtfully over his vaser. Finally, he pushed Dewlod's impertinent question from his mind and focused on the answer he had been given.

"Okay. Ralf, open a hailing frequency."

"Check, Captain." Ralf deftly tugged a nearby lever to its lowest position.

"Preparing to eject water reservoir tank," intoned the computer.

Ralf quickly returned the lever to its original position. He tapped his lips repeatedly with his left index finger. He adjusted another, nearby lever. A crackling noise seeped from behind a blackened speaker grille atop the Bridge's main viewscreen.

"Ah, there you go, Captain," smiled Ralf.

"Fine." Weyn addressed the viewing screen. "THREE DAY WEEKEND... this is the ship within visual range... Prepare to transmit us the exact interior co-ordinates of your cargo. Do not attempt to resist us, and you will be not be harmed. We do not lie. Otherwise, your ship and crew will be annihilated. THREE DAY WEEKEND, respond immediately!"

Despite his strident tone, Weyn seemed unusually calm and happily expectant. He nonchalantly scratched the itchy burns under his partly charred beard.

The main viewscreen flashed white, and then seemed to zoom out as an image formed there. An impressive martianoid figure sat on a throne-like command chair. The pale face remained impassive, then its nose twitched. It gave a deep sigh. Its claw-like fingers pulled it forward toward the viewscreen. It raised a finger to its lips, and began to flap them madly.

"Pppppppplllllllllll," was what was issued from the grilled speaker. Then, a peal of manic laughter.

The image faded, and the viewscreen was blank.

Weyn closed his mouth after a few moments.

"Helm Officer," said Weyn thoughtfully, "scan their cargo section and transfer the data to Ralf."

Dewlod silently performed this task.

"Analysis, Science Officer?" Weyn looked to Ralf.

"Looks like about 40 megagrams," mused Ralf.

"I don't mean mass. I mean content! Are they carrying the small arms?"

"Oh, uh." Ralf studied the console in front of him in search of answers. "No. They seem to have a cargo of, um. It looks like Martian THC sprouts and Belaznian spores, actually."

"Say, that's worth even more than small arms!" Weyn smiled broadly and his eyebrows quirked happily, "Hail them again!"

Ralf raised them after a few seconds.

"THREE DAY WEEKEND, prepare to give us your cargo co-ordinates or you will be boarded and your crew killed, slowly and painfully. You have fifteen seconds to respond." Weyn's eyes shone with excitement.

"We're probably gonna have to kill them," Weyn asided to Dewlod, unconsciously rubbing his hands together. Dewlod gave a lopsided and menacing smile in return.

The viewscreen flashed white. The same impressive figure appeared. It removed something black and silver from the clamp of its jaws, and handed the object off screen.

"Hi there!" it blurted enthusiastically, as it waved

and exhaled a giant puff of smoke.

"You're the Captain of the THREE DAY WEEKEND?" asked Weyn.

"You bet! Call me Mick. Glad to meet ya." Mick extended one hand towards the screen, but it banged against the glass lens, and Mick gave a long, unrestrained laugh.

"We want your cargo. Either give us the exact displacer co-ordinates, or prepare to be boarded."

"What? Hey, well sure. Come on over- there's lots for everybody. Who says you don't meet new people in deep space?" Mick laughed intensely again.

"I don't think you understand. If we board you, we will kill all of your crew, and you. Then take your cargo and blast your ship till it's holey enough for Nora's junkyard, marsboy," Weyn smiled at his own pun and pejorative.

"Are you threatening me, or something?" asked Mick, suddenly sombre. His face now glistened with sweat, and beads of perspiration began to drip off his chin.

"No, I'm just explaining how you are about to die, Kduimlian licker," snarled Weyn.

Mick blinked heavily several times, then his face contorted.

"Oh yeah? Well I don't like you!"

Weyn casually waved an obscene finger combination towards the viewscreen. Mick looked shocked.

"Oh yeah?" screamed Mick. "Well, eat it! Eat it raw!"

The viewscreen went blank.

"Looks like we will be boarding the THREE DAY WEEKEND," shrugged Weyn, quite satisfied with how the raid was progressing. "Halfnose," Weyn addressed his First Mate, Halfnose Swash. "You got a team picked out to board the THREE DAY WEEKEND?"

"Oh yes Captain. I've got a fine team picked out, fine loyal men, sir." Halfnose winked at Dewlod.

"Okay," Weyn puzzled momentarily over Halfnose's choice of words. "Get them displaced now. Let's get this done."

"Right." Halfnose snatched up his pirate action-tracking clipboard and exited the Bridge.

Chapter 5. The Time of the Great Cheese

The Zin team to board the THREE DAY WEEKEND had been chosen by Halfnose, under the advice of Dewlod. It consisted entirely of crew who would not have supported the mutineers. Once these killploys were off-ship, the mutineers would have no great problem in snatching Weyn's power.

With the pirate boarding party deeply involved in the slaughter of the THREE DAY WEEKEND's crew, Weyn disappeared into his living quarters to watch reruns of 'Space Family Cheesemonger' on video microcassettes, as he always did during the parts of a raid when his presence was not absolutely required. Weyn was slumped in a plush recliner, facing an enormous video screen. Voices spoke in urgent tones from behind the screen.

"Yes, son. There's something wrong with this planet. Somehow the cheddar have turned against us. They've attacked, and kidnapped Sue Beth."

"Oh gosh, Dad."

"Yes, son. I always knew that one day the cheeses would revolt. I never figured it would be the cheddar though. They've always been our friends."

"Oh gosh, Dad."

"Yes, son. I guess there are just some things we'll never understand."

The intense dialogue of the show was interrupted as the proximity alarm for Weyn's door buzzed. He reluctantly slapped the pause button on his video unit and spun his recliner around to face the door.

As it opened, Ratsy Nimoy, one of Weyn's newest recruits, staggered in and slapped the close/lock button behind him.

"What's the meaning of this interruption, Ratsy?" bellowed the Captain, in full rage mode.

"Captain! I've got to tell you- there's a plot, a mutiny! Dewlod Pretze has conspired to take over the GARGOYLE! Right now, he and the others are on their way to your quarters- to kill you!"

"Why are you telling me this? What do you want?" Weyn's eyes narrowed in suspicion.

Ratsy Nimoy flapped his hands with verbal inability. "Nothing, I am a loyal Zin pirate. I only want to continue with you as Captain of the GARGOYLE. I am attempting to be an honourable Zin!"

Weyn pondered this for a moment, then pulled out his vaser and used it to discorporate Ratsy.

"You have succeeded in being a fool, and that is all," stated Weyn. Ratsy's remains smouldered weakly in reply.

Weyn's door buzzed again, and Weyn opened it without thinking of possible assassins. Ralf made a cheerful greeting and stepped inside.

"Gee, Weyn, I never realized Zin ships like this had a games room. You wanna come down and play a few rounds of 'Mangle-a-Rabitt' with me? I've been practising all afternoon and..." Ralf's words trailed off as he noticed the steaming puddle on Weyn's floor.

"More insubordination?" guessed Ralf.

"Yeah." Weyn suddenly grabbed Ralf by the shoulder. "Listen, we've got to get out of here. My crew is mutinying."

Ralf flapped his mouth silently for a bit, then, "What are you gonna do?"

"Take the hyper-shuttle and get the Noraville out of here. You can come if you want."

Ralf shrugged. "Well, sure. I really don't want to stay here with some new Captain."

"That's what I figured."

=

Dewlod Pretze was having a beautiful day. All of the non-mutinous GARGOYLE personnel were trapped aboard the THREE DAY WEEKEND. The GARGOYLE now contained only mutineers, Gwer Weyn, Ralf, and a few neutrals from food services. Just to put the frosting on his beautiful day cake, Dewlod Pretze had ordered three of his most ill-humoured men to seek out the Captain, who was still loose on the GARGOYLE, and kill him. Ralf would share the Captain's fate.

Chapter 6. Clockwork Storage

Gwer motioned Ralf through a passageway, past an airtight door. They were in an enormous grey sheet-metal cavity towards the tail of the GARGOYLE. Throughout the cavernous area, small shuttles were parked at odd angles, seemingly at random.

"I've never been in this part of the ship before," confided Ralf, his voice tinged with awe.

"Yeah, well. It's the hangar area. We'll take the hyper-shuttle."

Ralf was about to make some bland affirmation of understanding when a voice cut through the air, questioning them as to their intentions. They both spun about to see a male technician in white overalls some five meters behind them. He reiterated his interrogative.

"Whaddya want?" Then, taking a closer look at the two beings, "Oh, sorry Captain, or should I call you Mr. Weyn now? I suppose you want a shuttle to try to escape in, right? Well, don't let me stop you. I'm neutral in this matter. I'm just down here cleaning the deep-fryers."

"That's fine." Weyn took another glance behind him. The sooner he could get off the GARGOYLE, the better his chance of surviving the mutiny. "Where's the shuttle with hyper capability?"

"You mean the FIRETONGUE?"

"Uh, yeah, whatever," nodded Weyn hastily.

"I could check the pizza delivery logs. That should give us the most recent info," said the unnamed food technician. Zin pirates often used their shuttles for pizza delivery during the off-season.

"Fine fine. Do it."

The technician ambled over to a nearby desk which was littered with data pods. After several seconds of rummaging among them, he selected a dated green data pod from the clutter. He blew on its top, but no dust flew into the air dramatically. He strolled back to where Weyn and Ralf waited, then pulled the data pod open.

"Should be listed here."

Weyn looked over his shoulder once more, and began to chew on his lower lip. Ralf looked earnestly at the technician.

"FEASTFILL, Fire Deck Lounge Special, ah, here it is. FIRETONGUE. So that would be two double pepperoni and a cheese cone."

"No, not their last order." Weyn suppressed an insult by swallowing hard. There was no time to lose. "The location! Where is it?"

"Of course. So, it should be in bay 11C. . ."

"And where is that?" snapped Weyn.

"Bay 11C, right next to the bay that had the fire last week."

"Where's-"

"Yup. It was but by the grace of Aron that we didn't lose a couple of shuttles with that one. And all because of McBeerson's witless work! I swear that guy can't do anything right. Since he's been assigned to my department I've had problems with him. I tell him to put the old pizza boxes in the shuttle's waste de-sizer and he winds up tearing the whole bloody aft compartment apart. I ask him what he's doing, and you know what he says?"

"What?" asked Ralf, while Weyn clamped his jaw and clenched his fists, squeezing the thumbs inside.

"He says 'I was just looking for the access hatch'! What a Kduimlian brain! He's always late coming back for lunch. He's always down the hall, or across the corridor when you need him. I've tried and I've tried hard, but no matter what I do, McBeerson simply won't learn. He won't listen. I talk at him all the time, all shift long, but he don't listen. He can't understand. I explain what I want from him- what I need from him- but he doesn't retain anything! He's more Terran than Zin! No Zin should be like that! Right?"

"I guess so," replied Ralf while Weyn sighed harshly.

"I've been the supervisor of food services for more than a sol now. That's more than the last two before me! I've seen them come, and I've seen them go, but this guy is simply not Zin pirate material. Last week's fire isn't my only reason for saying it. This's been going on a long time!"

"There!" screamed Weyn as he stepped forward and grabbed the technician by the shoulders. "There I agree with you, my friend!"

"You do?"

"Aron's eyeballs, yes!" affirmed Weyn as he released the man. He pulled out his vaser and aimed it at the babbler's face. "Yes, this has been going on far far too long. Now, where's the FIRETONGUE?"

"Uh-uh-uh..." the loquacious technician's speech was now impeded by burgeoning stress.

"Where," croaked Weyn, his face scarlet, and his aim beginning to tremble.

"Bay 11C! Bay 11C!"

"And where the Noraville is that?"

"Just-" the supervisor gestured to his left "-down there. Five bays down."

"Thank you so very much." Weyn fired his weapon into the supervisor's open mouth. His throat charred open, and he fell to the floor, thrashing in pain. Ralf's face was very pale as he looked upon the mortally wounded Zin, but Weyn was striding away towards where the FIRETONGUE reportedly was. Ralf had to run to catch up.

=

Ship's Log 1969.038-1805   Captain Dewlod Pretze recording:
An hour ago, the THREE DAY WEEKEND cargo was

displaced to our cargo area. We then destroyed the ship, and with it those elements of the GARGOYLE crew aligned with Weyn. One Neinsarch missile was used. Being that a Neinsarch explosion causes a rift in the dimensional fabric, and is readily detected by Space Patrol, I have ordered the GARGOYLE to leave the area at Warp 18. Our forced haste causes us to abandon any attempt at tracing our missing shuttle (the FIRETONGUE) through hyperspace. 'Captain' Weyn and that mass of martiancy, Ralf, may have escaped my direct vengeance, but their deaths are ensured. If the actual Neinsarch detonation didn't killed them, then the dimensional rift will place them where death is inevitable.

Crew Status: No losses since the THREE DAY WEEKEND was destroyed. I've arranged a meeting of all upper ranking crew for later today. There are some promotions and some dismissals to be made. (Internal note: have some commendations printed up, and make sure my vaser hand weapon is fully charged.)

Chapter 7. Hop, Skip, and a Thump

Gwer Weyn sat at the helm of the FIRETONGUE, typing data into the shuttle's navitron, reading the codes on the data pods spat out through little slots in the control panel, and then repeating the process. Ralf stood behind him, waiting and hoping for the moment when the Zin pirate would hurl the ship into the safety of hyperspace.

Just as Weyn was about to grasp a freshly extruded data pod, a huge vibration shook the shuttle. Both he and Ralf were momentarily blinded by the flare of intense orange light that passed through the only modestly filtered view port in front of them.

"Somebody blew up the universe!" moaned Ralf as soon as his vision recovered.

Weyn didn't quite agree with Ralf's assertion, but mentally acknowledged that that was indeed how it appeared. From his seated position at the helm, Weyn could see approximately 100 degrees around the front of the shuttle. Where formerly he had seen stars, nebulae, and various constellations, he now saw nothing. All that remained was the cold void of eternally solemn space.

A deep voice boomed out of the darkness: "Shuttle of the fourth planet of the system Aquillenn! Homeland of Reyio the Magnificent! Life-blood of the peoples who are to populate the worlds of Garrtenameni, Bebop, Yyrytiliom, Dklumm, and Pud! Follow me to the universe of Tssarofentiasterogliss! Your quest for Evrlife has begun! Rejoice!"

"How's that again?" Ralf's eyebrows furled.

"Just shut up and follow me," replied Jrrak, Great God of the Universe of Tssarofentiasterogliss.

"Forget it!" interrupted Weyn. "Listen you, you put those stars back right now! You may not realize this, you're messing with Zin, and you don't mess with Zin!" Weyn thrust his chin forward obstinately.

The FIRETONGUE lurched, unseating both occupants. Weyn tried to claw himself back towards the control stick. He managed to grab it, but it felt loose and disconnected in his hands.

The shuttle began to manoeuvre independently of Weyn's control stick gyrations. He continued to struggle with the stick tenaciously, but ineffectively, as the shuttle flashed through multiple unknown galaxies, and perhaps, universes.

Finally, the sensations of colour and time variation were too much for the two mortals. They fell into unconsciousness.

=

When Weyn became aware of his surroundings again, he was looking out the front port of the FIRETONGUE. He saw neither normal star configurations nor solid black void, but rather what appeared to be a translucent bluish green mist. He wondered where he had seen that mist before. Then a fish swam by.

Weyn turned to Ralf, who was still curled into a fetal ball in the co-pilot's chair, and sputtered for a moment before being able to inquire "Do you see that?"

"Yeah," Ralf nodded, partially unwinding. "Somehow we wound up with a voyage to the bottom of the sea."

"Ha ha ha," stated Weyn matter-of-factly. "This is serious."

"Are you sure?"

Weyn looked down at his keyboard. He punched in a question, waited a moment for the data pod to emit, then grabbed it, pulled it open, and read the answer.

"Yes. I'm sure."

A moment later, Weyn had formulated his plan of action. He tried it out on Ralf:

"Look, this is our only chance: we use the airlock as a sea-lock. We use our pressure suits as deep sea diving equipment, and we do our best to get to the surface, however far above us it may be. Every one for himself. How's that sound?"

"Sounds okay, I guess," shrugged Ralf uncertainly.

The two immediately moved to the 'suit lockers and began stuffing themselves inside the 'suits provided there. Of course, they were two sizes too small. That is, Weyn's 'suit was two sizes too small for him, and Ralf was two sizes too small for his 'suit. When they finally judged themselves properly attired, they hopped into the 'sea-lock' and allowed the seawater in.

=

Space Patrol Report 1969.038-1712   Captain Siso Sbor recording:

A Neinsarch explosion has occurred in the Cannus Fens sector of space (between the stars Oris and Lymur). Being the nearest Space Patrol Scout, the STARSLAMMER has been dispatched to investigate. Attached are photos of the resulting dimensional aberration, and data on physical characteristics of same. There are no Friggian ships, nor reports of Friggian attacks in the area. Therefore, the most obvious explanation is that the explosion is the result of pirate actions. No further data is available. My ensign wants it officially noted that the dimensional aberration is pink in colour. The significance of this escapes me.

Chapter 8. Planetfall

Weyn watched Ralf from his seated position on the beach. His 'suit lay on the beach beside him. Moments earlier, he had pulled himself out of the 'suit, and carelessly tossed it aside.

Clad simply in a Zin tunic, with a vaser pistol in his left front pocket, Weyn relaxed as he watched Ralf struggle in the water some ten meters from shore.

The FIRETONGUE had not sunk to the bottom of some deep ocean as Weyn had originally feared. Rather, it lay beached twenty meters from the shore. The water only covered the lower two-thirds of the shuttle.

Weyn sneered with amusement as Ralf's head surfaced again. Every few moments, the dull grey helmet would bob above the surface, Ralf would take a few unsteady steps, fall again, and finally re-surface. He had already taken about ten minutes to get half way to shore.

Ralf could feel Weyn's pitiless eyes upon him as he continued to struggle towards the shore. A memory of the first day aboard Weyn's previous ship, and how Weyn had humiliated him then, returned to Ralf: after a raid on a small colony within a system located at the near edge of the Milky Way Galaxy, Weyn had brought Ralf to a room with a dying Fornaxite, an inter-galactic being.

These large blob-like beings have one big eye-pouch housing dozens of eyes, and a belly covered with various appendages of unknown function.

Weyn indicated that this colonist needed first aid, and Ralf should rhythmically pull on the largest appendage, a dark-purple lance with a cluster of needle-like spines at the end. After several minutes of strenuous yanking, it was clear the being had already expired.

As Weyn commiserated with Ralf. The rest of the crew seemed oddly jovial at this sad turn of events.

Several ship cycles later, however, Ralf had stumbled onto some of the crew watching a multi-species pornographic video which clearly showed the sexual function of the Fornaxian appendage. Then he understood the crew's earlier amusement at his 'resuscitation' efforts.

Ralf took another five minutes to complete the journey to the shore. Eventually, Weyn stood up, put his hands on his hips, clearly impatient waiting for Ralf to be ready to move on. Just before reaching Weyn, Ralf stumbled again and sprawled on the sand. Without attempting to get up, he pulled off the helmet and crawled out of the 'suit.

"I thought I'd never make it," said Ralf, squinting through the bright, sunshine on the alien planet.

"Me too." agreed Weyn.

"You had trouble getting ashore too?"

"No. I also thought you'd never make it. Let's go."

With the Zin's rough helping hand, Ralf was on his feet again.

The beach extended fifteen meters from the shoreline, before it abutted lush tropics. The large yellow sun was forty five degrees off the horizon as they headed inland.

Pushing their way past obstructing vegetation, progress was slow. Half-meter wide leaves hung from insect-laden trees. Grass underfoot was unusually dark green and fine. In some spots, the grass thrived so thick that a foot would sink several cm into it before finding solid purchase.

They encountered no problems with animals. The only organisms they spotted, besides insects, were large birds and turtle-like creatures. The small black turtloids seemed content to congregate around tree bottoms for communal bark chewing, while the large multicoloured birds preferred resting in the trees singing songs resembling four brash electro-pop tunes played simultaneously but equidistantly out of phase at twice the normal speed.

After they had travelled for an hour, the big sun's position was thirty degrees above the horizon, and Weyn surmised it was getting late in the day.

It was then that they reached the first sign of civilization. It read 'Mont: 4 si'. Beside the sign, a winding trail disappeared into the thick landscape.

They followed the path until the big sun touched the edge of the horizon. At that point they must have travelled '4 si', as they had reached Mont.

A large circular open space surrounded by buildings made of stone, and flanked on two sides by clusters of smaller buildings made of breezy walls woven from cane-like wood strips. That was Mont.

Luckily, there appeared to be a pub in town. Weyn and Ralf headed for the only two-storey stone structure. The front door was an arch, as were the windows. This gave it an quasi-medieval style.

With only a cursory glance toward the 'Maimed Budgie Saloon' sign hanging overhead, Weyn gave the beads hanging in the entrance a decisive snap of the wrist, and lead Ralf into the dimly lit interior.

As their eyes adjusted to the low light level, the bartender directly ahead of them solidified. He stood well behind the bar, leisurely wiping a glass mug. The half dozen patrons and the bartender all appeared non-alien, in fact, completely martianoid.

Weyn stepped up to the bar.

"O bartender, we are travellers from a distant land. Long have we trodden this day. In the spirit of fraternity, and for the karmic redemption for this fair village of Mont, would you spare us a small portion of liquid sustenance with which we might slake our thirst?"

"No handouts for tourists, buddy," said the unsmiling bartender.

Just as Weyn and Ralf were about to step outside to rework their strategy, one of the other patrons approached them.

"Did I hear you say you are travellers from a distant land?" inquired a wrinkled male dressed in an equally wrinkly, shabby white robe.

"That's right."

"Bartender!" The wrinkled male motioned. "Two 'Mole and Sons' meads for my friends. If I may introduce myself... I am Ginus, the village sage."

"Village sage?" echoed Ralf, looking to the bartender.

"We couldn't afford a village idiot," deadpanned the barman as he held his a drinking vessel up to check for smudges.

Ginus ignored the remark.

"Do tell me of your travels," he bade them.

"It's a long story..." said Weyn, looking uneasy.

The bartender delivered the liquid refreshments, and both off-worlders took an opening gulp.

Ralf hiccuped twice, then blurted, "We're on the quest for Evrlife!"

Weyn looked at Ralf in horrified wonder.

"Evrlife..." nodded the sage. "I have knowledge of that quest."

"Ginus, I've told you before. Don't mess with my customers!" snarled the bartender.

"Quiet, fool!" thundered Ginus. "Do not attempt to interfere with the imparting of divine illumination! Gentlemen, have you knowledge of the destination of your journey?"

Ralf shook his head.

"I thought not." Ginus leaned closer to them. "You must travel to the Forest of 1000 Names, then pass beyond the Newart Mountains, through the Esie pass. Once you have done that, you will find your destiny just beyond the Plateau of Eternal Illumination."

The Zin stared skeptically at the aged sage.

"Will you remember these directions?"

"Oh, I'll remember them," shrugged Weyn.

"Okay. You have a long journey ahead of you, my friends. Bartender, some food for my most worthy Evrlife seekers!"

A few minutes passed, and the requested food was served. Roasted turtle-creatures. The meat was tough and harsh, made appealing only through the liberal use of sweet and sour sauce. Ralf had one small carcass, while Weyn, playing the part of the Eternal Glutton (Editor's note: not to be confused with the Eternal Hero), had six.

With feasting complete, the two weary travellers crossed the open circular area of central Mont, and registered at the Holiday Inn Express.

Despite the famous name of the hotel, they found the glasses in their room to be inadequate. Also, Weyn was a little ticked off to learn there was no ice machine on their floor.

At 2:00 AM, a wondrous vision came to both the intrepid travellers. The vision took the form of a majestic and charismatic god dressed in purple robes and a heavenly crown of living sentient jewels.

The great vision spoke to them thusly: "Ah! My children! You have done well! Soon, so very soon, you shall come to the immortal land of the origin of Brekop the Tall. There you will find your seeking's fortune. Along with that: the great gift of Evrlife! Rejoice! Oh, and don't try to steal any of the towels; I'll be watching you."

Ralf awoke in a cold sweat. He unpacked the towels and hung them back up in the bath.

Chapter 9. Troll Troubles' Terrible Toll

Just before the first sun rose, Weyn and Ralf checked out of their hotel room. Their decision to travel to the Forest of 1000 Names was hindered only by the fact that they knew not where that region lay. To clear this up, they stopped the first person they came upon in the street. The conversation was swift and fruitful.

"Wanna banapple?" asked the native Montian.

"No no. Could you just tell us how to get to the Forest of 1000 Names?" asked Weyn.

"Sure."

"How do we get to the Forest of 1000 Names?"

"Round about half day's travel due south."

"South?"

The Montian pointed.

"Thank you."

=

South of Mont, the land began to gently slope upwards. The ground became drier, abandoning the classification tropical and trending towards desert. The vegetation also changed. Rather than the even spread of short bushes and small trees, they encountered small oases of tall trees and large areas where dry ground substituted for flora.

Two hours later, dry ground predominated. They had entered a parched land of endless unsaleable tracts of sand covered with scorching sunlight. They met gaunt men, seemingly teetering on the precipice between life and death. These men called themselves 'real estate agents'. They also encountered obese air conditioning salesmen sporting platinum-capped teeth.

When a half-day of travel had passed, the landscape began to rebound from its barrenness. Soil replaced sand, and eventually, housed green life. Birdsong again became commonplace.

When they came to a wooden bridge crossing a small river, Ralf called out in jest, "O bridge trolls, may we cross?"

"No!" came a defiant shout.

Ralf was suddenly knocked over as a small swarm of trolls rushed out from under the bridge. Weyn levelled his vaser and began to vaporize the nearest ones.

One stubborn troll already had his teeth settled in Ralf's leg. Ralf began to kick wildly, trying to shake it off. He didn't manage that, but in his frenzy he did knock most of the other trolls into the river where they drowned.

"Look at that, Weyn! Some kinda bridge trolls these are! They can't even swim!"

Weyn didn't answer; he had other things to do. He was wildly stabbing an especially tenacious troll in the eyes. The troll didn't seem to notice this, as he was in the process of digesting one of Weyn's elbows.

As two trolls jumped Ralf, he ducked. Each of the two tricky trolls tried to tear the other to threads. Ralf casually shoved them towards the river. Splash.

The only remaining troll was the one still lodged on Weyn's elbow. Weyn finally managed to get his vaser against the hairy creature's skull. As he depressed the trigger, the troll's head popped with a loud original sound effect (perhaps, blwooof!).

Ralf groaned. "Sure glad the scoundrels couldn't swim."

"Yes yes. Don't dawdle. Let's leave this loathsome lair of lifelessness."

"Lethal loathsome lair of lifelessness?"

"As you like."

They left. Almost.

"Halt hun-like ones!" cried a tall martianoid male who appeared to be carrying approximately fifty unoccupied troll leashes. "You have terminated my trolls! By choosing to roam this riverbed for recreation with my personable pets, I have discovered as dastardly a deed as ever dealt!"

"Shut-up, silly senile supercilious slob!" yelled Weyn.

"Slime," muttered the troll-walker.

"Grr," growled Gwer, as he again demonstrated his delight with his weapon of destruction (blwooof!).

The troll-walker's lifeless body fell to the ground. Blood bubbled beneath his burns and blackened bones. Bleah!

"Reeeeettttcccch!" retched Ralf wretchedly.

They moved on, and soon the River of Alliteration was behind them, and their consonants had returned to a random selection.

Chapter 10. War Of The Words

Before another hour of trudgery passed, Weyn and Ralf did reach the Forest of 1000 Names. The grassy plain ended abruptly with a wall of immense dark green trees. The forest was sufficiently dense to reduce the light level within substantially.

At this point, the big sun was again touching the horizon, so they stopped in anticipation of the coming night.

Weyn had gathered some dead branches from the forest floor and was heaping them in a small clearing.

"Are those edible?" asked Ralf.

"Dead branches. For a fire. It'll get cold again tonight."

"A fire? You're going to ignite things on purpose??"

"Ralf, I'm a Zin pirate. I don't get all weird about combustion."

"Don't you care about the carbon content of this planet's atmosphere?"

"No," declared Weyn.

With the advance of anti-gravity and bacter technology hundreds of sols ago, Mars and most of the Alliance had long moved away from all types of fire, or 'uncontrolled ignition' as they termed it.

Combustion of any matter was considered anti-social, and an affront to natural beauty. Petroleum was used solely for lubrication; wood, for construction. Youth Scout survival skills included setting up a solar transducer in bright, dry areas, or a BacterVolt surface in darker, wet areas.

Weyn's campfire began to smoke, and then to crackle. He grunted in satisfaction, and pulled a small, dead turtle from a pocket. He quickly rigged up a spit to suspend the turtle over the fire, and then settled back to watch its progress.

"You know, the Alliance has a lot of stupid ideas. Idealizing peace and harmony is manipulative. There's only peace and harmony when the population is controlled. Zin don't like to be controlled."

"The values are meant to encourage beauty and happiness for all," explained Ralf.

"It's a joke. Only the rich are happy, and they get to decide everything. We Zin choose our own destiny. We don't live somebody else's second-hand life. Beauty is a fake idea. There is no beauty, only desire. Beauty is just what we call something before we discover it is worthless. Of course, I like the Joy part. That's a worthy value. Peace and Harmony, you can keep them."

Ralf couldn't argue with Weyn. He was too mesmerized by the dancing flames of the uncontrolled ignition in his midst. The tiny bit of turtle that Weyn allowed Ralf seemed to be more about demonstrating his skill as a survivalist, rather than sustaining his travel partner.

"So, do we have time for this? Why not just find a ship and get off this backward planet?" asked Ralf.

"Now who is unlovely?" chided Weyn. "No Ralf, opportunity is something Zin recognize. Once we have Evrlife there will be lots of time."

=

The next morning, after moving less than a hundred meters from their camp, they were attacked and captured by a group of pre-industrial warriors. The painted-faced, spear-carrying bunch bound their prisoners' hands, and herded them back to their settlement to be incarcerated in a small grass hut.

The guards tied Weyn and Ralf to the pole in the center of the hut, then remained posted outside the door. Quite soon, a representative of authority came to interrogate them.

"Names?" demanded the loin-clothed tribesman

who held a rustic bark-clad clipboard.

"Gwer Weyn, Zin pirate, adventurer and warrior extraordinaire, dashing sexual predator of four galaxies, working on five, fearless defender of self, unsurpassed champion-"

"Two As in Weyn, right?" their interrogator was already rubbing the clipboard with a spit-wet thumb, as if to correct what was previously noted.

"Two As?!" Weyn was outraged.

"Thought so. And you?"

"I'm Ralf."

"One A. Check." Their interrogator licked his lips and made an audible tap on his clipboard for a period.

"Okay, onto the important stuff. What's the name of this forest, Waayn?"

"That's Weyn. I don't know. I should be asking you that."

"Ignorance is no excuse for not knowing." The interrogator backhanded Weyn hard across the face. "The Name, please."

"Forest of 1000 Names?"

He slapped Weyn again. "That is a blasphemy of a name- it is not The Name. Tell me The Name."

"Why don't you ask him?" Weyn nodded towards Ralf.

Their interrogator looked towards Ralf, put one hand on his hip, arched an eyebrow, and then returned his glance to Weyn.

"Get serious."

"Look, we just want to travel through this place peacefully. We don't care what it's called."

This enraged their interrogator.

"Would you conduct business with a man whose name you didn't know? Marry a woman? Buy a hunting gopher?!"

"Hunting gopher??"

"Okay, okay. Maybe a hunting gopher." Their

95

questioner shook his head. "But don't tell me you would enter a land without knowing its name."

"Let's say the name of the forest is Treelandia," argued Weyn. "What does that prove?"

"That proves you do not know The Name, and you are our foe. You must now die."

"Wait! Whoa there! So we don't know the name! That doesn't mean we're foes!"

"All those not of this tribe call our forest by a wrong name. All those are our foes. They must die, as you must."

"Why are they your enemies?" asked Ralf.

"They battle us, and refuse to submit to The Name,"

"I don't understand," stalled Weyn. "You fight over a name?"

"We are idealists," shrugged their interrogator. "You got a better reason?"

"But we will submit to The Name," said Ralf softly.

"Y-y-y-you," stammered their interrogator. He shook his head violently, and then fled the hut.

=

After their interrogator's exit, Weyn remained icily silent. It was quite apparent to Ralf that his contribution to the conversation with their interrogator had not been fully appreciated. He resolved to refrain from making any more comments until he and Weyn were once again safely on their quest.

In any case, reflected Ralf, Weyn generally handles people much better than I.

Ralf had not even begun his attempt to reestablish relations with Weyn when another forest dweller entered the hut. This one was more nearly clothed. A flowing black robe hung around his body. The sleeves were flared with gold and silver sequins on the edges.

"Well afternoon to you, I am Elder Lowm. You are Ralf and Waayn?"

"That's Weyn and Ralf!" asserted Weyn.

"Mmmhmm. And what is the name of this forest?"

"We've been through all this! We don't know the name of your bloody forest. We're travellers, not residents," spat Weyn.

"As I thought." Elder Lowm nodded to himself. "Savages, travelling as wild animals. It's not often we stumble upon the likes of you. The policy in such a case is quite old, being devised by an elder many generations ago."

"What's the policy?" asked Ralf.

"Automatic execution."

"Oh, nice question, Ralf. Smart question." Weyn rolled his eyes. Ralf's merely widened.

"The problem could be solved quite simply. You're not citizens of any other forest tribe, are you?"

"No."

"Well. You could become citizens of our tribe, and you could learn the proper name of our forest" explained Elder Lowm. "I, personally, have never used the execution clause. It's something I'd like to avoid."

"Yeah, that's something we'd sort of like to avoid, too," agreed Ralf.

Elder Lowm and Weyn looked curiously at Ralf.

"Why don't we become citizens, then?" asked Weyn.

"It's not that easy. You either have to be born here, or perform a boon."

"A boon? We can do a boon. What's a boon?" asked, stated, and questioned Weyn.

"It's a favour beneficial to my society. Something that would earn you a place among my people."

"No problem. That's what we'll do then. Name your boon!" Weyn gave his best gregarious smile, and Elder Lowm took a step backward and unconsciously placed his hand on the ceremonial dagger sheathed near his thigh.

"I'm not sure you understand. Boons are not

something like... like fixing us brunch. They are dangerous undertakings."

"Not more dangerous an undertaking than an execution, I trust?" said Ralf, feeling snide since his earlier attempts in the conversation had been under-appreciated.

Weyn and Lowm gave him another curious glance before the Elder continued.

"I met with the Council just before I came here. We've decided on your boon." They waited for Lowm to complete the thought. He didn't.

"This is for you," he said instead, and reached under his cloak. He handed Weyn a fist-sized silver rock. One band of intricate carvings encircled it. "You will head towards where our forest meets the Newart Mountains. There, in a cavern set deep within the heart of those mountains, lies the home of Adept the Sorcerer. He will make the Adelphius Boon speak." Lowm motioned open-palmed at the rock. "Thus you will learn your boon. It may seem roundabout to send you to Adept with the Adelphius Boon, but there is a reason. I would advise you to earnestly try to convince him to assist you with your boon, otherwise failure is a great probability."

"Right. Very good." Weyn pocketed the Adelphius Boon. "We'll be off then. I like to get an early start on these boons."

The pirate began to slowly edge towards the hut's opening. "You have a real nice day, Elder Lowm, and hopefully we'll see you again in a few days..."

"Waayn..." sighed the Elder, as the Zin suddenly sprinted towards the exit, but bounced off the chest of a two-meter-plus tall forest dweller. "I believe I've neglected to introduce you to your travelling companion. Ralf, Waayn, this is Rip; Rip, Ralf and Waayn."

"How do you do," said Ralf as he stepped forward

to shake Rip's hand.

"Rip rip?" the victim of massive hormonal imbalance gutturally questioned, as he speculatively looked down at Ralf's small hand entrapped in his.

"No, Rip. Just shake it, like this."

Lowm demonstrated with air.

Rip gave it a try, but lifted Ralf's feet off the ground and then caused him to land indelicately on his knees. Ralf made a noise like a puppy with its tail caught in a cleaning drone.

"Rip will see to it that you return here after your boon is complete. And only after your boon is complete," smiled the Elder.

"Marvy," enthused Weyn, as Ralf began to pick the gravel out of his
kneecaps.

Chapter 11. River Slow, Mountain Wide

Travelling with Rip turned out to be a lesson in logic manipulated by the limited intellect. The forest dweller refused to detour around natural obstacles, such as rivers and lakes.

The Crimson Equal Sign swimming lessons Weyn had taken early in life now became an essential skill.

As for Ralf, the muscles in his upper arms were becoming well-toned. After all, clutching a hairy native's neck and being dragged through a lake is no stroll through a park.

Discussion of their navigational difficulties was impeded by Rip's minuscule vocabulary.

"Rip, this way. We're going around the lake," Weyn would attempt to explain.

"No. Adept!" Rip would point across the lake.

"A little detour would save us lots of time."

Then Rip would become frustrated, blubber "Rip rip" in quick couplets, and interject "Adept!" with a violent directional gesture every now and then.

At that point, Weyn would usually do his fiendishly authentic impression of a feline Meowite about to strike, and Ralf would follow up with some such inanely mollifying comment as "Well, it is a Thursday."

Travelling with Rip was gruelling, but swift. In less than a two days, the threesome had progressed from just entering the forest to nearly leaving it. Where the land sloped upward to hint at the Newark Mountains, the forest thinned, then abruptly ended.

After only an hour travelling up the slope, they came to the entrance of the sorcerer's cavern abode.

The slit-like aberration was covered with moss and, as Ralf noted with surprise, small insects resembling rabbits. Weyn's reaction was typical of a Zin faced with the unusual: denial followed by rage and contempt.

"What?! Well, I don't see them. That can't be. Nora's belly! This is an ugly planet!" A Zin grunt of contempt, and Rip led them deeper into the cave.

"Good day!" shouted a youngish male martianoid wearing a t-shirt emblazoned with 'Chevy' who had appeared amid the shadows of the labyrinth.

"How can you tell from in there?" asked Ralf.

"Do you realize you have rabbit-bugs crawling all over your, um, outer port?" asked Weyn, blinking his eyes rapidly in an attempt to have them adjust to the low lighting conditions sooner.

"Of course," said the young man from his peacock chair. "They're my pets. I lessened their size in order to make feeding them easier."

"You can do that?" awed Ralf.

"I'm Adept the Sorcerer! I can do anything. So I'm told."

"Then why don't you just increase the size of the food?" pushed Weyn.

Adept glared at him. "If I did that, you'd ask me why I didn't shrink the rabbits, no? Even a child could come up with a question like that."

Weyn flexed his neck muscles.

=

Weyn could not follow Elder Lowm's advice to seek Adept's help with their boon as he, after two days of being Adept's guest, still had not discovered the nature of that boon.

Adept had provided them with sleeping accommodations, food, drink, even access to his large movie library; but each time Weyn brought the Adelphius Boon out, Adept would change the subject by telling anecdotes about a cloud-worshipping culture he had once wizarded.

In a characteristic moment of boredom and tranquility in Adept's cave, Ralf and Rip sat watching a remake of 'The Lewd Potato Chip' (that classic psychological thriller) while Weyn sat alone in one of the inner chambers, cleaning his toenails with a comb.

That morning, Adept had finally given Weyn a concrete reason for his not yet making the Adelphius Boon speak. He wished to delay that event in order to 'influence a specific order of events not necessarily natural to this time-line'. To explain what he meant by this explanation, he had illuminated them as to his true nature.

"I am not a wizard, in any metaphysical sense. There is no metaphysical sense, only metaphysical nonsense. I am a traveller through time and across the divide of possibility. I have seen many dimensions, many peoples. I have been a citizen in over a thousand civilizations, with parking tickets outstanding in perhaps half of these. My powers are not those of a magical wizard. I am but a borrower of technologies, an acquirer of knowledge. I am neither immortal, nor deity. The one thing that I am, that is Adept."

Weyn and Ralf found this explanation fascinating. It hadn't explained Adept's explanation any, but it was kinda neat anyhow.

Now, apparently, the impediment not actually clarified in his excuse had disappeared, for Adept approached Ralf and inquired about Weyn and the Adelphius Boon.

"Weyn? Yeah, he's got the boon rock. I think he's doing a Zin hygiene rite inside one of the deeper chambers."

The Zin treated their hygiene in a religious manner, that is to say, only on Wednesdays.

"Do you think he's free?" asked Adept.

"No," shrugged Ralf, "but he's real cheap." Ralf curled up and convulsed with giggles.

"Right." Adept nodded and smiled at Ralf.

Over the past few days, Adept had noticed that Ralf

had begun building a defence mechanism utilizing humour. When previously Ralf had just looked down at the floor when the Zin overruled his simplest decision, now Ralf tossed back a thin pun, or some form of snide comment. Somewhere Ralf had gotten the idea that it was not the natural order of things that he should be dominated effortlessly.

Humour, thought Adept, is a sign of ego, or at least a slight conception of self worth.

He was amazed the tide had turned so definitively for Ralf. The few days of isolation in his cave, with just the four of them, had shown Ralf his own passivity. Perhaps the realization was half the cure.

Weyn's impatience for the Adelphius Boon to speak outweighed any annoyance he felt at his hygiene rite being disturbed. He hastily, and without complaint, followed Adept back to the main chamber where the others waited. All four gathered around a large round table.

Without comment, Weyn placed the Boon in the center. Adept felt for the two small indentations on the lateral ends of the Boon, then inserted a metal stick in each. A slight buzz ruffled the air, and the Boon glowed with energy.

"Adelphius Boon... 37842 Boon A..." a receptionist-type voice emanated from the silver sphere. "For the last five seasons, the village in the Forest of 1003 Names has been scourged and damned by a hideous creature of unknown origin. Over one hundred young warriors have been defiled by the beast. Many snatched from their homes, disappearing as their huts are destroyed by another of the commonplace rampages of this monster, a foul creature that stands tall as a Graythor tree, moves with the speed of a Kalisiu bird and reeks of Clearasil. It is worse than a Zin in personal cleanliness, but refuses to tolerate acne.

This creature must be destroyed in order to preserve

the harmony and idyllic nature of our village. To perform this duty is a boon, Adelphius Boon... 37842 Boon A."

The glow within the sphere diminished, then disappeared.

"Looks like you got the 'kill the Beast of Barsom' boon," noted Adept. "That's too bad. It's one of the tougher ones."

"Elder Lowm led us to believe that you might be of some help in completing our boon," hinted Weyn.

"Why do you want to do this boon, anyway?"

"We have to. It'll give us citizenship, which will let us have free passage through the forest."

"But you've already have free passage." Adept spread out his arms in an expansive gesture, "My cave is beyond the edge of this forest."

"It's not that easy."

Adept raised his eyebrows inquiringly. Nobody was looking at Rip. After a few moments of silence, Rip began to emit low rumbling sounds in his thick neck, perhaps self consciously, or in anticipation of the revelation of his true status among the three travellers.

Adept caught on.

"Did the villagers send him along with you?" Adept's shoulders twitched as he resorted to his lowest form of self-indulgent antisocial behavior: he laughed at them.

Flicking an index finger briefly towards Weyn, he said "I thought he was your son!"

"Hey, I've only been on this planet a few days!" complained Weyn, his thoughts inadvertently wandering back to other times this declaration had been made, and the child support payment demands that had ensued.

"Well, if that's the only problem..."

Adept pulled a small oblong device from his side and pointed it at Rip. The monstrous native was too slow to avoid this surprise aggression.

The object shone blue, and Rip's eyes grew coldly blue. His body shimmered with an ill-defined aura of the same colour. The light turned orange, then purple, then red, then green, white, yellow, pink, the gamut of visible colour flickered through the object in an ever-accelerating rainbow promenade.

As the light engulfed him, Rip initially felt a tranquility, a mellow acceptance of past, present, and future. This seemed to continue for a time so interminable, that Rip was gripped by a deep physical need for movement, action, anything to shatter the void calm. Anger at his condition achieved this. This feeling mutated into stark fury, raw aggressive instinct. As the colours flicked by, so did each exaggerated version of Rip's emotions. Raw desire, unbridled lust was next. That was pretty fun. Then he moved into ecstasy. A joy so singing that the term 'singing joy' was but the yawn of eating an non-buttered dirtseed muffin. Hate, pity, hope, envy, impatience, love, courage, disgust, fear: the spectrum was run, and exhausted.

"Problem solved." Adept snatched the Adelphius Boon in one hand, and tossed it casually into a wooden rabbit-shaped trash container.

Rip stood motionless, eyes glazed and fixed on some space ahead of him. He had no will to move, to think, to feel. Reality was an anti-climatic inconvenience. Physiological depression ran rampant through his body.

Adept turned to the other two.

"Before you leave, there's something I must ask of both of you, and I think you owe me an honest answer."

Weyn looked uncomfortable.

"Weyn, who do you love?"

"Being a Zin!" shouted Weyn triumphantly, pumping one hand in the air, not realizing he had answered the wrong question.

"Hum. Okay. And Ralf. Who do you hate?"

"No one!" squeaked Ralf defensively.

"As I thought." Adept smiled in a self-congratulatory manner.

"Except maybe..." began Ralf, "talk show hosts who sing on their own shows."

Adept's smile briefly faltered.

Being such an advanced and sophisticated life form, Adept was not prone to cliché-filled goodbyes.

He gave them each a small gift: Weyn, a premium bottle of dandruff shampoo, and Ralf, the small oblong device he had used on Rip. Then Adept smiled, and turned away.

Chapter 12. The Big Empty

As Weyn and Ralf trekked into the Esie pass which cuts through the Newart Mountains, Weyn reflected on the advice the village sage at Mont had given him. They faced but one last danger, one last obstacle before their quest for Evrlife was complete. They had to traverse the Plateau of Eternal Illumination.

The idea of sleep was thrust aside and they bristled impatiently for the climax of their journey. Small chubby birds chirping sharp flute-inspired riffs circled above them, unseen, except as occasional shapes glimpsed against the starscape. Ahead, in the far distance, the horizon began to glow yellow-orange.

Dawn neared, and finally they could see their ultimate obstacle.

=

Marked against the weak pre-dawn light was a brilliantly lit strip of flat land. Hundreds of bright threads, silvery anti-gravity beams, stretched upwards every dozen meters or so forming extended lines along each side of the plain, and in clusters throughout. Far across the high elevation plain, they could see another line, the final one, of the brilliant beams reaching skyward. Atop these oddities swelled huge pods of fiery energy which each seemed to possess distinctly dynamic features and variations in colour. Were they alive?

To avoid detection, Weyn and Ralf moved towards the plateau with the hunched-over lope of a schoolboy having broken his first window. The orbs noticed them anyway, but as their culture had neither schools nor windows simply believed the strangers had acute back conditions.

Zin delusions of inter-dimensional persecutions

notwithstanding, the orbs continued to ignore them while Weyn and Ralf progressed across the plateau.

About halfway across, one of the orbs appeared to sense the interlopers and react. The anti-gravity beam upon which it sat unexpectedly dropped to coffee table height. The orb was suddenly in close proximity to Ralf, and began to cast thoughts into Ralf's head:

"Stay in school... Don't get married too young... Do you really need to buy that now?"

Ralf started to consider these advice, but instead resolutely forced his attention back to his intended path.

A set of orbs had also descended to block Weyn.

"Don't listen to them!" Ralf screamed. "Just keep going no matter what!"

"Think before you act... make sure you know what you are doing... consider the impact of your actions on others..."

Ralf was about half way across the plateau.

"Don't give rides to strangers... Never open an email attachment you were not expecting... there is no free lunch..."

"Aaaaah!" Ralf screamed across the final boundary, beyond the orbs, but Weyn was still somewhat behind.

Two orbs blocked his way.

"Never trust a prisoner with a weapon... Win people's respect by instilling fear in them... never give a sucker an even break..."

Apparently Zin illumination differed from Terran.

"Never pull a punch... there are no second chances... A wounded enemy is a dangerous enemy..."

The Zin's feet did an innovative new form of the double backwards zigzag as he weaved his way through the particularly dense cluster of orbs. Suddenly, he was past them all.

"Didn't want to wait, huh?" grunted Weyn as he tripped over the edge of the plateau and fell clumsily beside Ralf.

"I was waiting..."

Weyn got to his feet without looking at Ralf.

"That was pretty fancy footwork you managed back there," Ralf rejoined, in order to smooth things over and make up for defending himself.

"Well yes, of course," snarled Weyn. "It's just another amazing skill of mine."

The duo moved on and Weyn continued to explain the inordinately difficult childhood training a Zin received which was required for survival, until the Plateau of Eternal Illumination was a patch of light on the horizon far behind them.

They travelled slowly, but now more easily. Over the crest of a small hill, and through a rounded depression, an almost-valley, the grassy texture of the ground remained steady. Mid-morning brought a healthy blue sky with few clouds, mere streaks against the perfect canvas of azure.

Evrlife came upon them without warning. One moment they were walking up a small rolling lump of land neatly labelled 'hill' in Martian vocabulary, and the next, they were struck by the awesome sight of Evrlife.

"O Temples of Aron," muttered Weyn as he stepped closer to the unbelievable sight. "Of grandeur, of splendour, I have heard of no quest to exceed what we have attained, my travel companion..."

Weyn spoke crisply and eloquently, proudly displaying the strange trait of the Zin by which their vocabulary and syntax greatly improve as they near the culmination of a quest.

Ralf did not respond. The sight was too emotion-evoking to allow his attention to wander. His eyes traced the huge blocks of ancient stone that had been carved by the unknown craftspeople of days long forgotten. His gaze moved along the metallic roof of the awesome structure, where orange and deepest blue neon tubing ran laced like a lunatic's spaghetti lunch leftovers, and down to the marvellously ornate iron gates, located just slightly above ground level of the towering cylindrical artifact.

As they began to move towards it, they didn't notice as a strange grindingly dramatic music sprang up in the background.

The electronically distorted chords came crashing faster and faster as they approached the gate. Composure within the music's melody faded, and became wilder as the tempo increased. Just a step from the gate, they stopped, and a high chord sustained for a long moment as they stood, apparently halted. The climatic crash of the final note and beat were simultaneously accompanied by a huge neon sign activating above the gate: "EVRLIFE"

A moment later, below that, a corollary in smaller letters also lit: "No One Under 18 Admitted."

"I hope you brought your ID," muttered Weyn as he moved forward. Ralf followed him through the gate, then stopped, waiting for his eyes to adjust to the darkness.

"Weyn..."

"See anything!?" snapped the Zin.

"No- yes. What is there to see?"

The two travellers stood just inside the gate. Dimly, they could make out the stone wall of the structure curving away into the distance. As far as they could see, the circular structure contained exactly what it was contained in. A huge plain of evenly textured grass.

"It's emp-" began Ralf, his words cut short by the impact of Weyn's hand across his face.

"Shut up."

Ralf then moved to step deeper into the darkness, and Weyn followed after him angrily, annoyed that he had not been the first one to step deeper into Evrlife. Five minutes later, the gateway behind them dissolved into dimness, and the two were out of enthusiasm. Ralf

110

flopped resignedly on the grass, and Weyn joined him.

"Aron's nipples," swore the Zin.

He examined his fingernails intently, undecided whether to sharpen them or just chew them off. He looked over to Ralf abruptly, in a manner which seemed to demand an explanation.

"I'm sorry," said Ralf, without knowing why. Weyn relaxed slightly, somewhat satisfied.

The pair sat motionless, and slowly sank deeper into the plush grass. Ralf fingered the small bruise on his face where Weyn had struck him, then closed his eyes to shut out the unavoidable reality of his situation.

A rending Zin snore sprang from Weyn's throat, and Ralf also soon gave in to fatigue.

Chapter 13. Flashsideward

Brilliant heat touched Ralf's forehead, and he awoke suddenly. About him, the grassy plain inside the structure had turned white with heat.

He leapt to his feet, as Weyn did, and immediately his sweat glands gave a wet spasm, drenching his clothes.

The brightness obliterated his vision, and he lost track of Weyn. Ralf clenched his eyes shut again, and at the edge of a swoon, he felt a vicious gale assail him.

The wind swept him off his feet and into an atmospheric tumult. Ralf's eyes were no longer closed. He watched with terrified fascination as his body whirled through clouds of geometric bric-a-brac.

The Evrlife structure, now far below, had suddenly shrunk to a small, maybe ten meter diameter, tower, with the grassy plain within being replaced by red carpeting throughout, with a bizarre art deco throne at the center.

Now Ralf was sitting upon that throne. The walls dropped away under the crimson carpeting, as the throne area rose until it sat atop the tower. Far below, a roaring frigid sea hid the foundation of the tower.

In the distance, Ralf could see a similar tower where, upon a similar throne, Gwer Weyn rested.

The Zin appeared to notice Ralf at that same moment, for he hopped off his throne, ran to the edge of his tower nearest Ralf, and began shouting Zin battle cries.

Across the sea, innumerable other towers stood; they were foggy, perhaps obscured by the spray of the sea below.

Ralf's hand again went to the bruise on the side of his face, tracing the outline of the tender spot. A thick scar began to ripen under his touch. Dry scar tissue scraped his fingertip as he rubbed.

This impossibility was joined by another: Ralf could see the scar rapidly forming, this being quite the feat as the scar was on his own cheek. He saw his eyes look unfocused off into space as he carefully felt the wound.

Ralf was conscious of the feelings of his body, his position on the throne, and the rough scab under his fingers, but he no longer was his body. He was an outsider, an observer of mystical spectacles unfolding.

Ralf observed. As his scar began to grow black, and fester. As he fell off the throne with a huge pain racking his head. As his wound split open and spat foul black liquid. Liquid that ran warmly over his hands, engulfing his sense of smell and invoking a rich nausea.

In the background, Zin battle cries were replaced by the dry sounds of a broadcaster reading sports scores. The liquid drained, yet the wound swelled, as if the more it drained, the more the wound festered.

It reached the size of a pregnant Kduimlian. Then the blackened globe of diseased flesh hanging from Ralf's head burst, splashing the wound's poison over the royal red carpet. A huge puddle formed. Ralf's figure slumped into the wetness, appearing unconscious.

But Ralf was only too conscious. He was not the failed circus performer, mangled and crumpled in the center ring, but instead the horrified spectator contemplating the phrasing of his ticket refund request.

The slumped figure in Ralf's vision stirred. The Ralf-form stood without effort, and opened his eyes, unleashing a tremendous blaze of rainbow jigsaw stroboscopic light. The detached Ralf suddenly felt himself drawn back to his original body, this thing that now seemed so alien. They accelerated towards each other, and collided, achieving unity.

Now Ralf stood in a black space, seeing nothing but the other Ralf before him, that which had been him, but was no longer.

"Who are you?" asked Ralf.

The figure smiled. He appeared identical to Ralf except for the burning directness of his gaze, and the small white scar on his cheek.

"I am the sum of your experience. I am the knife that cuts a path through time easily and smoothly: I leave no jagged edge, and no doubt. I am the sum of your experience, yet am I unjustly hidden. I am the gut reaction to all your life lived in a single moment."

The figure paused, and reached to touch the fresh white line on its cheek.

"I am he who is struck, and yet is healed in the knowledge that I will heal and grow stronger for the healing." This Other-Ralf's hand passed over its scar, which promptly vanished.

"But who are you?" pressed Ralf.

The figure smiled enigmatically, and handed Ralf what appeared to be a large textbook which had just popped into existence behind the Other-Ralf's back. Ralf glanced at the title: 'How Not to Be a Jerk, and Listen When Someone is Trying to Explain Something to You, Kid.'

When Ralf glanced back up, the Other-Ralf had gone. Ralf was now looking onto a stage with four martianoid musicians gleefully pounding out a funky blues tune.

An overweight black male sat at a non-electric keyboard. He wore dark glasses and a bright smile. A hairless drummer and a musician with an upright bass stood in the background.

The fourth musician had shaggy long hair and moved back and forth between the keyboardist and the other two as he played his glossy black guitar.

He winked at Ralf.

The ceiling in the room was quite low. There were lights just above the stage, but they were shrouded in smoke. Obviously this was a low dive Martian nightclub, complete with the usual assorted patronage of the bored, the losers, the intoxicated, the curious, and the odd economy plan tourist in basic idiot off-planet uniform: obscure baseball cap, plaid orange/green terry towel shirt, grubby white knee length pants and ankle length sneakers revealing no socks.

The keyboardist sang in a richly deep voice, as his hands bounced up and down along the range of keys:

Hate is the venom baby
Love is the antidote
If you ain't been sick brother
You ain't better yet

Then Ralf was with his father, Agmewobbialluyllsesmeecolysion. Once again he was a young boy on his home planet, Terra. Ralf stood, with his head cowed, er, bowed, before his father's desk as he received his usual weekly bit of profound advice. His father's study was an austere and functional place, with incomprehensible volumes lining two walls.

"What you must realize, before you attempt any action," his father droned on in the ever calm voice of the over-experienced, "is this simple yet transcendentally universal maxim: no one knows, and what is more, no one cares."

Ralf misinterpreted this as he misinterpreted everything his father told him. He took this advice as a simple statement of unalterable reality, rather than the warning needed to protect youthful enthusiasm from premature deterioration, which instead was intended. His father's study disappeared in a flash and...

Ralf saw a huge mass of primitive Martians bowing to a statue of a stylized warrior god. He saw them offer a sacrifice of fresh lasagna. They performed ceremonies consisting of rote movements, dances, incantations, invocations...

... and Ralf was running through crowded streets. Peoples from all cultures glancing off his hastening elbows. Storefronts of various enterprises flowed past. The food markets, the program stores, and of course the borderline illicit establishments promising hot and spicy entertainment: Venusian Cajun restaurants.

Dusk came in an instant, and Ralf's panic faded. He slowed his pace and found himself among the throng congesting an open air market. A great many voices drummed against his ears. They were the calls of the criers for the market shops, each extolling the necessity of some item.

One voice caught Ralf's attention.

"That's right folks, you'll never know how you managed without it. With the De-doubtifyer you'll move through decisions easy as you move through a temple on a Thursday morning. Yes, you'll finally be free from all those unwanted influences which cause so much strain in your life! Not only will it do that for you, but with this inexpensive item, you'll find the peace and tranquility of Easy Living that you all deserve so richly. And even that's not all! For a limited time, we're also offering you this special bonus gift...!"

The man leaning into the microphone from his raised platform handed the De-doubtifyer to his assistant, who promptly laid the gizmo, a pair of modified spectacles with opaque shields protruding laterally to narrow the user's field of vision, onto a small table.

"For no additional charge, you will receive a pair of our universally famous Extendo-lips. These are not available in stores! Millions of these beauties have already been sold for 9.95 each, and now we're offering these for no cost when you purchase the amazing De-doubtifyer!"

The man held a pair of wax lips up close to his own. With a scissor-like motion he closed his thumb to his index finger. The wax lips extended on two pieces of crisscrossing plastic to a length about eight cm distant from his face.

"Suitable for use with great aunts, or for those of you whose marriage has reached the stage where simple physical affection no longer defines your love. So step right up! My assistant will be accepting personal cheques, MasterDisk, Martian Express, Cruncher's Club, and of course, cash. Supplies are limited, so don't wait and get left out! Believe me, these items are unbelievable. That's right folks, you'll never know how you managed without it! With the De-doubtifyer, you'll move through decisions easy as..."

... and Ralf was once more in the smoky nightclub. This time the band was playing a hardcore ultra-speed electronic waltz. An almost sanitary Ejsaanon, obviously recently wiped down, grabbed Ralf and whirled him away in dance. Ralf noticed that embossed on the front of the band's drum kit was the name 'Aron'...

... and Ralf was in the Chamber of Arbitrary Social Justice, the primary ruling body of the Alliance. He watched in stunned wonder as men of great wisdom and power moved slowly about the chamber, speaking a few, lean, meaningful sentences to one another, and rolling dice.

... and the Thing was sloshing at Ralf, who turned and ran, a conspicuously wise decision on his part. Down a corridor, into an access tube, up another corridor, from the width of the NOSFERATU, to the breadth of the NOSFERATU, and all about the depth of the NOSFERATU, until finally, at the tail section, as his corridor finally came to an end, Ralf turned to face It.

Its terrible sucking tormenting the air, Ralf was pulled towards the hideous tree-creature. As his head was engulfed by one of Its deadly branches, Ralf felt a tremendous pressure squeeze his cranium, increasing inexorably, until his skull bones audibly snapped, caving in and spilling grey and white neural matter into the waiting stomach of the Thing...

"Aron!" screamed Ralf, and he was once again on the evenly textured plain of grass in the Evrlife artifact. Had he merely been sleeping? Weyn was.

"Weyn! Weyn!" Ralf violently shook his Zin companion.

"What?" asked Weyn, still half asleep.

"Evrlife is upon us!" cried Ralf.

"Correct you are!" stated a thick, bass voice. "I am Jrrak, Great God of the Universe Tssarofentiasterogliss!"

The unlikely Evrlife tower dissolved into a dark and misty nighttime landscape of nothingness as Jrrak continued.

"You have shown me that I have indeed chosen the correct entity for the unsurpassed gift of Evrlife!"

Jrrak smiled and raised his hands as if to deliver a ritual benediction. The black sky rumbled, and flares of sheet lightning lit random patches of night behind Jrrak.

"Stand!" the Great God commanded.

Ralf scrambled to his feet.

"Throughout the millennia, I have searched for the right individual to bestow this infinite gift upon. Now, through these tests, I see that I truly have found my messiah!"

"Messiah!? What Kduimlian spittle is this??" demanded a distraught Weyn.

"I mean the gift of Evrlife will be bestowed upon the being who is going to save these universes! Not merely my own universe of Tssarofentiasterogliss, but also Rordehtoeiglidokuhny, Gwelopwanneidlottipshietse and Bip!! The gift of Evrlife is the ultimate in power! Its possessor will obtain the seven powerful powers, plus eternal life! He will be the saviour of everyone and everything, everywhere!! Now is the time for the transference of

Evrlife! Step forward and accept the gift, O Chosen One!!!"

Ralf stepped triumphantly forward.

"I, Ralf, son of Agmewobbialluyllsesmeecolysion, proudly claim the gift of Evrlife as my own. From this day forward my eternal life shall be devoted to the salvation of this and, uh, all universes as stated by Jrrak. My cause shall be with all peoples and all planets of all solar systems throughout all galaxies of all universes in this dimension, with the statutory exception of those beyond any door sill whose height exceeds six centimeters! Let my ascendance to Evrlife be NOW!!"

"Uh, Ralf..." Jrrak rolled his eyes. "Sorry old boy. I didn't mean you. I meant him!" Jrrak pointed pointedly at Weyn.

"Sorry." Ralf and his florescent red face took a step backwards.

Gwer Weyn stepped triumphantly forward.

"I, Gwer Weyn, son of Spike Weyn, proudly claim the gift of Evrlife as my own. From this day forward my eternal life shall be devoted to the salvation of this and all universes in the dimension, as stated by Jrrak just now. My cause shall be with all peoples and all planets of all solar systems throughout all galaxies of all universes in this dimension, with the statutory exception of those beyond any door sill whose height exceeds six centimeters! Let my ascendance to Evrlife be NOW!!"

"Evrlife!" screamed Jrrak.

Weyn was enveloped in a swath of luminous energy arcs. Intense swirls of colour and sound pulsed throughout the huge, roofless chamber. The air was filled with an immense, almost infinite, sound which transcended all minds and languages in translation. The air grew unbearably hot, and then rapidly dropped to a temperature which Ralf had not previously thought possible. Weyn was lifted upon a column of dazzling light. Upwards he glided, almost disappearing into the atmospheric ether, until finally the column cracked with a display of what appeared to be, but what Ralf knew could not be, vaser fire.

Then, Weyn the Eternal was gone.

"Well kid, I'll be seeing you," said Jrrak, and was also gone.

Ralf stood alone in the Chamber of Evrlife. He could not fully grasp what he had just seen, but he intuited that someday, someday in the far future, his wiser future self would still be completely and utterly baffled.

Book 3. Jammy Handtrickes Redux

No one knows, and what is more,
no one cares.
If it works, don't fix it.
On even the longest journey,
the first step is always quite near your left foot.

- from The Three Axioms Of Aron
[The Complete Dunderhead's Audio Guide To Aronist
Dogma
< Vinyl Source Z002 >]

Dramatis Personae

Terry Aaronstrum (Terran)
Musician/Artist

Clokene Daggr (Martian)
Alliance Intelligence Analyst

Hass Haisenbreyer (Martian)
Space Corps Colonel

Klick Hipdip (Zedeezian)
Sub-Commodore, Space City C-0004

Redek Hunnish (Belaznian)
Space Corps Rear Admiral

Myelin Jaylo (Delaroug)
Space Patrol Ensign, STARSLAMMER

Knuckles de Klowne (Martian)
BOTCH supervisor

Doctor Mahad (Ihnewian)
Research scientist, Space City C-0004

Sir Phiddeus Phuddel (Martian)
Member, Chamber of Arbitrary Social Justice

Mary Poncherelli (Martian)
Space Patrol General

Slasic Tetraham (Martian)
Alliance Senator

Chapter 1. Grapes Of Writhe

C aptain Sbor sat at the command position of her
charge, the Space Patrol Craft STARSLAMMER.
Listening through a set of small foamy earphones, she
reviewed her ship's logs of the last few weeks, admiring
the calculated tone of her calm yet stentorian voice.

Sbor thought whatever she had to enter in the log,
be it records of civilian deaths, senseless piracy acts,
interplanetary skirmishes, no matter how dire the
situation, she always managed to sound as if she were
reading the all-natural ingredients of a new breakfast
cereal on a video advertisement.

But it didn't really sound like that.

Sbor had reviewed to 1969.036 when the reminder
timer alerted her the first log entry of her day was due.
The Captain of the two-officer patrol ship flicked the
switch to cut her log review, and flicked another to
initiate the daily log recording process.

Leaning back into the squeaky command chair, she
linked her hands behind her head, stretched, extended
her feet to rest on the shoulders of Myelin, her
subordinate and lowly ensign, and once entirely settled
and comfortable, began to dictate today's ingredients
into the microphone.

=

*Space Patrol Report 1969.046-0902   Captain Siso
Sbor recording:*
STARSLAMMER is presently in dry dock at Space
City C-0001 for her semi-annual systems check and
BacterVolt paint touch-ups. Half its crew will board the
Space City for shore leave. The remainder of the crew
are to remain on the ship assisting with the systems
check. Morale is at a satisfactory level.

At 1969.045-2250, the STARSLAMMER
encountered a small shuttle holding a decaying orbit

around the neutron star R22M07P78. The shuttle did not respond to hails, and so was removed from orbit and forcibly docked with the STARSLAMMER.

A single male martianoid occupant was recovered, unconscious, and subsequently identified as Ralf, are eh elle eff, a Space Corps officer who has been missing and presumed dead since the CargoShip NOSFERATU was destroyed on 1969.032. The shuttle was marked as FIRETONGUE, purportedly a transit for a larger ship named GARGOYLE. Our records contain no such names as interstellar or even interplanetary craft.

Upon further investigation, it was found that the shuttle was actually the 'DORA DENISE', a transit missing since its mothership 'SMITH FAMILY ADVENTURE' was attacked and destroyed by Zin pirates almost two sols ago.

Ralf has been placed under arrest, being charged with Grand Theft Spacecraft for lack of a better explanation of his evident criminal activities. Of course, it is possible he was kidnapped. An investigation continues.

=

Space City C-0001 orbited the planet Mars. Like other space cities, it was the stop-over point and loading dock for its planet. The assortment of interstellar and intergalactic vehicles that found profit in stopping at Mars were rarely the sort of vehicles to actually land on a planet. Because of this, they required a location to drop off and pick up cargo, and a place where space-weary crew could escape the confines of their ship.

Each space city fulfilled this function efficiently. They all provided cargo holding services, and a link with planetary communication networks. Some of the major cities provided near space-resort style recreational facilities: fine cuisine, plush lodging, theatre, cinema, and nightclubs.

In one of those nightclubs, namely an establishment presented as 'The Luminescent Jelly Bean Video Arcade and Olde Time Pub' by means of thick neon strands on its weathered polystyrene exterior, an important decision was occurring.

The event transpired in a dimly lit corner of the pub section of the enterprise. A small plastic table, as scarred with smoke-stick burns as the face of a pubescent Martian is generously ladled with traumatic skin disorders, housed two portly government officials. Not your basic government officials - the genus and species of government official whose contract negotiations meet the public eye round about the time said documents have been filed and already accumulated four mm of fully approved and sub-committeed Alliance dust. Top government officials.

"But who? Who would, who could-" the first official said, as if he were pondering the identity of the mystery killer whose revealing on last night's episode of 'Value-packed Suspense Stories and Endless Spy Movie Sequels for the Insomnia Stricken' he had missed because his dog had suddenly developed a case of hysterical priapism and had to be rushed to its therapist.

"Someone we can trust not to aroo us ascround- er, that is," muttered the other, peering through the thick haze of intoxication that seemed to be more a part of the actual establishment's atmosphere than a result of its products.

"A courier, that's too simple, something like this, it's not for civilian hands..."

"No! That's right," nodded the other sloppily. "This is a job for the military!" A fist thumped the table to stress the point. A hollow sound resulted.

"And yet, by the High Priestesses, if we get some simple striped flunky, you know, the ones with the thick barrel-like chests... the medals... the hoarse voices. Always barking things like 'tenshun!!'

The first man coughed a chuckle, which prompted the other to continue, in a louder voice. "Ten hut! Preeeeee-zent arms!!"

This continued for a few minutes and eventually escalated into one of the officials goose-stepping around the bar barking stylized military manoeuvre commands, and the other doing an inadequate job at containing spasms of hilarity.

Soon, a bouncer stepped over, roared 'Dismissed!', and illustrated.

In an alley off the Crimson Illumination Lane, an important decision was occurring. Two heavily intoxicated, although now somewhat mellowed, top government officials tossed ideas back and forth in a fine example of a superior political brainstorming session:

"I think I'm gonna be sick."

"My wife's gonna kill me."

"Slasic, where the Nora is my car?"

"That depends where we are..."

"We're across the lane from Voorti's House of Boorishly Wine Sodden Golden Moments."

"Shall we?"

=

The next day, decision still undecided, Senator Slasic Tetraham was being crushed alive by a huge cranial pressure commonly known as a hangover.

He asked of his personal secretary but two tasks: first, to bring him three anti-inflammatory pills; and second, to bring him the file of Space Corps special agent Rael Ephe.

Not being in top form herself, as she had spent all night playing Acoustic Toothpick for a local band called The Voidheads, Tetraham's personal secretary screwed both these duties up. She brought him three Diethene tabs (powerful euphorics), and the file of

Ralf, an inactive Space Corps science officer.

Three hours later, Senator Tetraham was in conference with several other top-level government officials. All areas of the political structure were represented: Space Patrol by General Poncherelli, Space Corps by Rear Admiral Hunnish, the domestic Martian government by several Presidential aides, and the central Alliance government by Sir Phuddel, a member of the Chamber of Arbitrary Social Justice.

Senator Tetraham was concluding his opening remarks:

"And so, my friends, it is quite clear that the situation would best be handled by an entourage of three, and for those of you with too much wisdom and too little memory, I'll name the chosen envoys again: Alliance intelligence analyst Clokene Daggr, who happens to be one of our foremost Aronist scholars, Space Corps Colonel Haisenbreyer, a man of indisputable judgment and loyalty, and Space Corps Science Officer Ralf. This group of skilled officials will transfer the artifact to the planet Aqua Posteri 8, where our Bureau of Transparency is situated. Any questions, gentlewoman and men?"

"Just one, Senator," said Sir Phuddel, leaning slightly forward over the conference table.

"Shoot," said Senator Tetraham, not noticing Admiral Hunnish's left hand unconsciously flick against his ceremonial vaser holster.

"I am quite familiar with Agent Daggr's history, as the Chamber has had need of her services in the past. Colonel Haisenbreyer I am also familiar with, as I'm sure all of you in this room are. One could hardly have overlooked his successful operations mopping up the remnant Martian pockets of the Covenant Sons two sols ago. Space Corps Science Officer Ralf, on the other hand, however, I am not entirely familiar with, that is to say..."

"Who is this Ralf person anyway?" interjected General Poncherelli from her rather relaxed position: chair pushed back to allow her feet to rest, crossed, on the meeting table, arms folded haphazardly across her chest.

Senator Tetraham smiled. Perhaps the very memory of his decision that afternoon, advised by three tabs of Diethene, touched off the pleasure center in his brain.

"Actually, it's only been quite recently that I've become aware of this most unusually talented Space Corps officer. On the advice of one of my top aides, I reviewed Ralf's file, and I was astounded by his quiet and yet awesomely important contributions to Space Corps.

Due to its highly classified status, you probably have not heard of this but, approximately one sol ago, when Alliance security was seriously threatened by an ethereal creature from another plane of existence named Herb-"

"There's a plane of existence named Herb?" quizzed General Poncherelli, still reclined with her head at a relaxed angle and eyes probing the ceiling.

"The creature," grinded Senator Tetraham. "The creature was named Herb."

"Oh. That makes sense. Not to me, but it makes sense."

"Anyhow, Herb had already attacked and destroyed two outlying colonies. Apparently he came from a plane of existence which exists through a paper/ink continuum, with a monotheistic metaphysical structure. The deity there, being a manic pulp mystery obsessive, continually manipulated or 'wrote' his universe with Herb in the middle of second-rate detective thrillers. Herb became quite desperate to escape, and when a little quantum randomness dropped a powerful talisman from the plane of Toyl King into his influence, he did escape.

With the talisman, he transformed our two colonies into four Harlequin romances and a full length feature called 'Teddy meets Zarva, the Solar Powered Gazelle'."

The Senator paused to see if he still had their attention. They stared back at him. He still had their attention.

"The Space Corps Destroyer CATBREATH was then dispatched to the area but the entire ship crew was killed, that is, translated by the talisman into a large volume called 'Lizards I Have Known'. All, except Ralf, who was serving his first tour of duty as a third class communications technician on that ship. Why Ralf wasn't absorbed into a prose form, we simply don't know."

He paused to see if they had any ideas why this would be so. They didn't.

"Herb had intended to commandeer the CATBREATH, as up until then he had been operating out of a small interplanetary shuttle, but when he boarded the CATBREATH, he was confronted by Ralf. Through some unconventional form of intuition, Ralf discovered that Herb's plane of existence contained no humour, except for the odd vaguely amusing epilogue.

As a stratagem, Ralf began to recite his favourite jokes. With 'what is black and white and red all over; a zebra with multiple stab wounds', Ralf forced the talisman out of Herb's tenacious clutch. With 'why did the duck cross the road; because it was stapled to the chicken', Herb's plans of universal domination collapsed and he slipped back to the alternate plane from whence he came..."

Senator Tetraham noticed the entire population of the room had assumed the body position earlier pioneered by General Poncherelli, From their reclined positions, they stared at him with pursed lips and raised eyebrows.

"And, uh, uh, Ralf was then taken off the CATBREATH and promoted to the position of science officer aboard the NOSFERATU."

Not a word from his audience.

"My top aide looked at his file and recommended him..."

The steady hum of air-circulation fans.

"Well, he comes from a very loyal and connected family..."

The senator's audience murmured indistinguishably.

"Who creates those reports, Senator? Where did that, er, documentation come from?" asked Rear Admiral Hunnish.

"Why the senior officer at the incident would file a report if there wasn't a log to be found which could explain the, uh, events taking place."

"In other words, you've got two empty Alliance colonies, one deserted Space Corps Destroyer, miscellaneous obscure literature, and Ralf's report."

"The report is signed," confirmed the Senator, as he leaned across the table and tipped the pages before Hunnish such that the others could all see the scrawl at the bottom of the pencilled foolscap page that was Ralf's report.

Admiral Hunnish smiled blandly at the Senator, and stood up.

"A most informative conference, Senator. I'll be sure to write this up in full in my log," Hunnish said, wondering if he had any Assassination Authorization forms back at the office.

The others got up one by one, patted the Senator on the head, and left.

Chapter 2. The One That Got Away

Captain Sbor was reviewing her favourite volume of the Alliance's statutes, the one concerning regulations and health standards for interstellar travelling menageries, when an order notification came in from her superiors aboard Space City C-0001.

A sallow colonel advised her that new orders were forthcoming, and broke the link scant milliseconds after she had acknowledged this fact, not allowing any of her usual argumentative rhetoric, challenging the motivation and origin of the order.

This was standard operating procedure for Sbor. Her appointment to the position of Captain had been due to this very procedure. The previous sol, when Sbor had been given an order by her former captain, she had picked it apart and found it involved shady dealings.

With two audio communications to superiors above her former captain, Sbor uncovered a scandal involving that former captain and several of her crew linking them with black market activities, or more specifically, to the smuggling of illustrated underwear to a strict Justice of Aron colony where such things were outlawed as being dangerous and prime symptoms of approaching cultural disintegration.

Sbor's self-righteous grin slipped as the ship's automatic order processor indicator flashed; the orders she had just received were being transmitted for storage to the internal ship log. The present had burst in on her. She pulled the data pod, and read her new official orders:

=

STARSLAMMER- Space Patrol Craft- 1969.047-0804.33511#
TO: Captain Siso Sbor
FROM: General Mary Poncherelli, Space Patrol HQ

(C-0001)
Immediately drop all charges against Space Corps
Officer Ralf and escort him to Central Space Terminal
at New West York. Complete orders soonest. Priority
13.

=

Sbor held the data pod with a double-fisted steely
grip. The verification code matched. It was authentic.
Her palm sweated and smudged the data pod screen.
Her lips tensed.

"Myelin!!" she screeched.

"Yes'm?" inquired her subordinate officer, flinching
in fear her Captain would blow up again as she had
done when they had been ordered into the
Spammelleum Conflict. It had taken weeks to get the
teeth marks out of her uniform.

"Myelin..." Now Sbor's voice trailed off in a
mysterious manner, much the same manner as the voice
of a member of the Covenant of the Sons of Aron trails
off when recalling the highly consoling verse from the
second of the '7 Holy Albums of Aron' reading:

> *It is okay*
> *Hey*
> *How could it be any other way*
> *Hey*
> *Could it turn from gold to grey*
> *Eh?*
> *In a solitary day*
> *Nay*
> *It is okay*
> *Hey*

Sbor radiated inner peace.

"Myelin..." she repeated speculatively.

"Yes'm?" repeated the Ensign.

"We have a drop off. Alter our orbit so we pass over
New West York."

"I'll program it right away, ma'am," replied Myelin,

not understanding why her Captain had suddenly become so pensive.

Sbor was an unpredictable officer. One moment she would be raving and ferocious, infected with anger, and the next moment, calm and collected as a tortoise realizing it need not worry about rent controls being lifted.

Sbor was indeed calmer now. She appeared almost happy, even relaxed, except that she was clutching a small microphone and speaking in hurried but hushed tones into her personal log. Her eyes darted about her surroundings. A smile formed on her lips briefly, involuntarily.

Sbor could smell another scandal ripening.

Chapter 3. Freedom is Another Word for Nothing Left to Lose

Ralf wandered the streets of New West York in a daze. His feet seemed to sense that he had no particular place to go, and expressed this knowledge by taking him along random patterns through the maze of streets.

He had been recently displaced from the grand, public New West York Central Space Terminal to the smaller, nondescript Space Corps Depot in the Pondlyn district where rushing out to greet and orient him was exactly no one. Now Ralf pondered his future.

He was dazed, more dazed than usual that is, for two reasons.

One: he was having a difficult time accepting the abrupt changes his life had recently slipped through. The Quest for Evrlife, a climax in itself of some rather hard to accept events, had been followed by a rescue that turned out to be an arrest. When Ralf had just begun to accept the fact that he might spend the rest of his life making identification plates for space vehicles, he was unexpectedly set free and tossed into the wild streets of New West York.

Second reason for being overly dazed: he had been mugged moments earlier. A coalition of muggers had set up a blockade at 52nd and Park Avenue and were methodically stopping all pedestrians and stripping them of liquid assets.

Ralf did not know his current status with Space Corps. Could he enter the nearest Space Corps branch and be posted to a ship, thus satisfying his daily needs for nourishment and video games, or would he be doomed to wander the dusty streets of the immense metropolis of New West York, forever scrounging for morsels of food, struggling to survive the direct onslaught of rush hour sidewalk traffic, destined to sleep in gutters and on mouldy park benches, his life the twisted and confused ruin of a man betrayed by his society, his life one rambling incoherent shuffling run-on sentence, much like this one, yet windier, in autumn?

These thoughts raced through his head. With bitter irony, he recalled how sols ago he had given up a secure and promising career as a magnetic pencil sales apprentice on the corner of 12th and Avenue C for the thrills and glory Space Corps had to offer.

Ralf quoted from the third scripture of the '7 Holy Albums of Aron':

The dimness of the hour
rushes over my earlobes
What sacredness in this body?
What primal mustiness enshrouds
the eye of the walrus?
O, what price these thrills?

Ralf could not imagine his situation deteriorating any further. Whimsical fortune, however, had a superior imagination.

As a black limousine sidled toward the curb near Ralf, two burly Martians hopped out and neatly kidnapped him. One of the chaps simply tucked Ralf under his left arm and, muffled cries aside, slid him soundlessly into the tomb-like back compartment of the sinister vehicle. The second kidnapper followed, and closed the vehicle door, leaving Ralf jammed between them.

The expensive and spotless vehicle glided through the streets of Pondlyn. In a few minutes they were over the Pondlyn Bridge, across the immense canal that cuts through New West York and into Marslem, another central district of the immense city.

They veered into an area of cramped and aged

streets that chopped the land into ridiculously small parcels of property. In this ancient part of the city, thousands of merchants were squeezed together into a dense commercial zone. The buildings were tiny, each containing an average of two merchant shops on the ground level and only a half dozen levels of residential condos above.

People moved quickly and seemingly purposefully down the sidewalks, taking large steps and tapping their hip pocket every third stride to check if their wallets were still intact.

The limousine circled a certain block once, then entered a small, multi-level concrete parking mall. They reached the putative bottom level, activated a large but nondescript metal door, and descended another level.

Ralf was not frightened. He had been to this place previously, this subterranean parkade and office complex, and he knew these people meant him no harm. At least no harm in the conventional sense of immediate physical damage.

This was BOTCH Headquarters, that super secret service performing duties that Space Corps and Space Patrol, each self-consciously scuffing their shoes in the dust under the public eye, could not.

With calm efficiency, the two kidnappers took Ralf directly to the office of Knuckles de Klowne, current head of BOTCH operations.

Now, for the second time, more than two sols later, Ralf again sat in this near mythic figure's office.

Knuckles de Klowne was an unusual figure for a BOTCH head. While the last grand supervisor, simply named T, had been an agent who had risen slowly through the ranks of the institution's shadowy command structure, Knuckles was known as a public prosecutor, but was actually a whiz-kid mole-handler, or asset conversion specialist, now labelled 'nouveau niche' among the secret cadre, as he had acquired his high ranking job as payback for a single spectacular spy sting.

Sols ago, he had acquired the then-current Terran Chief Administrator Agmewobbialluyllsesmeecolysion (or Agme, as his friends called him) and encouraged him to pioneer Terran rights throughout the Alliance, this at a time when it had been more than unfashionable to do so.

Despite vicious attacks by powerful right wing groups, Agme had carried out the organizing of major reforms. Some of his peers and fellow radicals were caught in mob situations or jailed. Some were murdered ruthlessly by anti-Terran terrorist groups. His group had shocked the public by splitting away from conventional Aronism to form the infamous Covenant of the Sons of Aron sect.

Of course, it was all a ruse. Agme was in the pay of the Martians, and was selling out Terran secrets and Terrans involved with fundamental Aronism. Once the Terran rebel movement had been thoroughly identified and hollowed out, Agme was rewarded two-fold: first he was given a cushy high-profile government job, better than the one he currently had, and second, his one remaining son's future was protected.

Knuckles de Klowne promised Agme that his son, Ralf, would be shielded from repercussions, and his expenses for private school first, and then Space Corps later, would be fully funded.

During the climax of the battle for Terran rights reform, Prosecutor de Klowne dropped out of sight, taking on his new role in BOTCH, and Agme was rewarded for his Martian loyalty with the position of Ultimate Senator, a role subordinate only to the members of the Chamber of Arbitrary Social Justice. His replacement, the new Terran Chief Administrator, was likewise a Martian mole, and soon quashed the pointy parts of the Terran reconciliation legislation.

These developments flashed through Ralf's head, just as they had more than a sol ago, the first time Ralf had met Knuckles de Klowne.

There and then, Ralf had been advised that his father was in fact a mole within the Terran movement, a government asset who had provided detailed intelligence on the Terran movement from within.

Ralf had felt some relief as he assumed his father's life of deceit and fear of exposure explained his cold and distant attitude. Also, it explained Ralf's fast track into Space Corps.

Ralf did not hate his father for betraying Terra because something had broken in the old man after the death of his first son, Seymour. Ralf remembered how his father had changed, had disappeared into his job. Just before the founding of the Covenant, Agme had sent his son to a private school on Mars, an elite school with a record number of Space Corps alumni graduates. No longer would Ralf sell magnetic pencils and live in his parents' basement.

When Agme had shared his plans for his son, Ralf was fearful and unenthusiastic. Ralf recalled the conversation.

"You will go to this school and make something of yourself!"

"What about my work in the magnetic pencil industry?"

"That's not a career! Magnetic pens are coming!! You can't spend your life in the basement playing Comets!"

"But I like the out-gassing!"

Despite his protests, Ralf was convinced to attend the Deimos School of Military Arts for his final sol of study, where he was one of the very few students already holding an admission agreement with Space Corps.

Ralf did not want to think about what further unpleasant truths might be revealed in Knuckle's office.

With a wave of his hand, Knuckles dismissed the two burly escorts from his office. With another wave of his hand, he motioned Ralf to seat himself in front of the large plastic desk.

Knuckles stared silently and intensely down at Ralf. His position, standing directly behind his desk, hands planted on the desk, leaning, domineeringly over that same desk, did not help to put Ralf at ease.

"You're wondering why you're here? Right?" asked the intense leaner.

"No. I know why," answered Ralf.

"You do, do you?"

"Yeah," said Ralf thoughtfully. "I'm here because those two burly chaps brought me here."

"Yes, but you're wondering why those two 'burly chaps' brought you here, right?"

"Well, no. I guess it's their job to do things like that."

"But why was that their job?"

"Maybe all the jobs as system analysts were filled," shrugged Ralf.

"Yes, but why were all the jobs for...uh.." Knuckles's words trailed off into an auditory void. He tapped his fist against his mouth for a moment, and looked even more intense.

"So," said Ralf. "What did you want to talk to me about?"

Knuckles stared at Ralf as if he would find it extremely pleasurable to use Ralf's epidermis to wrap fish. He eventually sat down wearily, and pulled a data pod from the tall pile of the flexible readables that covered one side of his desk.

"Ralf," he said without looking up from the open data pod, "Do you believe in Aron?"

"Mm-hmm."

"What would you do if you knew that the Final Weekend of Ugly Judgments and Just Beautiful Irony was rapidly approaching?"

"Go back to my hometown and tell off Mrs. Blackheart."

"Mrs. Blackheart?"

"My level 2 education instructor."

"I see," said Knuckles, not biting. "Well, what would you say if I told you Aron didn't exist?"

Ralf stared blankly at him. "How do you know?"

Knuckles smiled. "Well, look at you."

Apparently Knuckles was asking all the questions, and giving no answers. Ralf wondered why he had been brought to Knuckles's office by the two burly chaps who couldn't find jobs as system analysts. Maybe it was some kind of a government make-work project. It didn't make sense, but that didn't disturb Ralf unduly as he had grown accustomed to being in situations that made no sense.

Knuckles handed Ralf a blue data pod.

"Here's your revised Space Corps identification, and your new orders. You've been promoted to Colonel for this assignment."

"Wow! Thank you. What assignment?"

Knuckles leaned back in his chair.

"It's very simple, actually. You'll be working with two others, analyst Clokene Daggr, and Colonel Haisenbreyer. It's a courier mission. You'll board the STARSLAMMER, travel to Space City C-0004 where you'll pick up a Aronist artifact. From there, the Scout Craft PLASMIC SURFER takes you to the planet Aqua Posteri 8, where you deliver the artifact to the Bureau of Transparency. All the details are in there."

Ralf glanced down at the blue data pod containing his orders.

"What kind of Aronist artifact is it? Like another album, a number eight to go with the '7 Holy Albums of Aron'?"

"No. Nothing like that. An exact description of the artifact can be found in your orders. There's also a carcass, a body. We believe it is the corpse of someone from Aronist times, that is, a person contemporaneous with Aron."

"A body? Wouldn't it be a little mouldy or something?" asked Ralf.

"It's in an airtight container. There may be some type of stasis equipment involved. The artifact is filled with other ancient materials besides the body," detailed Knuckles.

"I don't understand one thing- why is BOTCH handling this? Why is this such a secret operation?" Ralf looked at Knuckles as if he realized he had asked a very rational, intelligent question, and was only mildly surprised at his sudden ability at this new activity.

"You remember the Covenant of the Sons of Aron?"

"I thought they were all arrested a while ago," recalled Ralf.

"Not all of them. Just the formal organization here on Mars. On Terra, few officially ever belonged to the Covenant, but the majority of martianoids on that planet are a great deal more fundamental with their Aronism, a great deal more inclined to interpret the '7 Holy Albums of Aron' in such a way as to believe their destiny is to rule the universe with an Aronist theocracy, unlike the rest of the Alliance who have a more reasonable, non-literal interpretation of the scripture poems. You've heard of the 'Earthling Crusades' several hundred sols ago, when all the Terrans got in an uproar over discovering the so-called lost Third Aronist Album on their own planet?"

"I am a Terran," Ralf reminded him.

Knuckles continued to Marsplain Terran history to Ralf.

"The Terrans interpreted the album in such a way as

143

to convince themselves that they were a chosen people, the planet chosen to bring peace and enlightenment to the universe. So they started a massive war.

They renamed themselves. They went from being called Terrans, a logical name, to Earthlings, a bizarre obscure name used in that third album.

They lost the war, of course, but for a couple of days they were quite a nuisance. The Alliance is not used to having bloody wars right next to Mars. Aron, that's the Capitol's backyard!"

"Not beautiful," offered Ralf.

"No, not beautiful at all." Knuckles stared down at his desk for a few moments. "The thing is, Ralf, the '7 Holy Albums of Aron' were discovered on Mars. Civilization on Mars dates back to the time of Aron. Mars is the Capital of the Alliance, the oldest remnant of martianoid life in the universe. Aron is Martian. He has to be."

"Six of the seven albums were found on Mars, so that says something," admitted Ralf.

"Yes, the six albums were found on Mars, but this newly discovered artifact was found on a small asteroid at a null gravity point between Terra and Luna, and it dates back at least to the time of Aron, when Mars was the only civilized planet in the universe. A time when Terra was not yet Mars-formed, as our history books assume it was sometime in the remote past, long before the Great Reset."

Ralf sat in silent ponder, wondering if he could grab a couple of headache pills as soon as he got out of Knuckles's office. Theology gave him migraines. One time he had caught a bad cold just by saying 'eschatological'.

"It is imperative to get the artifact away from that location, and safely to the Bureau of Transparency on Aqua Posteri 8 where it can be studied in secrecy. I know your work, Ralf. Just over a sol ago, when we

144

needed someone to confront the extra-dimensional creature named Herb, I wasn't sure you could handle the mission. But you didn't fail then, and I'm sure you won't fail now. Remember, Ralf, total secrecy is our creed."

Knuckles extended his hand in a parting gesture of courtesy. Ralf shook his hand, being careful to use a firm, yet not overly aggressive grip.

"You can count on me," Ralf assured him.

"Sounds like we can count on each other, then."

Knuckles gave Ralf a confidently warm parting smile, and watched him exit.

The clandestine listening device in his desk then transmitted, via compressed data squirt, the latest audio activity in Knuckles's office to Ambassador Mauve Riggler's war room in the nearby Embassy of the Supreme Purple Worm, a highly organized and advanced society which formed the third leg in the local tri-galactic area balance of power between the Alliance and the Friggians.

The Supreme Purple Worm's officer on duty reviewed the discussion, scrambled his voicephone, and then contacted four major news-poders, two interstellar video news services, and his friend Guido (who has a very big mouth). He informed them all, in a digitally anonymized voice, that an ancient Aronist artifact was being kept under a heavy shroud of government secrecy on Space City C-0004, and could likely trigger Alliance instability, if not another Mars-Terra war.

Chapter 4. The Usual Suspect

Captain Sbor was pleased with her latest orders. Transporting three important and hush-hush delegates to a nearby Space City was a wonderful chance to network, or perhaps sniff out any scandals or illegalities concerning their affairs. The destination: the Terra-orbiting Space City C-0004. Elapsed time available for schmoozing and scandal sniffing: four hours.

Sbor met the freshly materialized threesome in the STARSLAMMER's displacer chamber.

"Most pleased to meet you," said Sbor as she reached out, shook Colonel Haisenbreyer's hand, and smiled formally.

"The pleasure is mine, Captain," replied the Colonel.

"And most pleased to meet you," said Sbor as she reached out, shook Clokene Daggr's hand, and smiled formally.

"A pleasure to make your acquaintance," replied Clokene.

"You.... you're..." said Sbor as she reached out, shook Ralf's hand with quick spasms of distaste, and smiled through clenched lips. She was having trouble with Ralf's sudden transition from alleged criminal to diplomatic envoy.

"Nice to see you again," noted Ralf.

The foursome remained silent as Sbor stared hard at Ralf and ran through her internal list of Alliance statutes concerning dress. She hoped Ralf had maliciously perpetrated an infraction and thus could be escorted to an appropriate stateroom, such as the brig. A few seconds elapsed, and still Sbor had nothing.

"Loathing to be hasty, but verily we must initiate study of the voluminous background data co-extant with our mission order information sheets forthwith," explained Clokene as she, with the other two, turned to exit the chamber.

"See you later," waved Ralf.

"Not if someone drives red hot spikes of rusty iron into your eyes," joked Sbor under her breath.

=

For the duration of the voyage to Space City C-0004, Ralf remained in the crew lounge with one other passenger the STARSLAMMER was carrying. As Ralf quickly discovered, the passenger was a roving reporter for the Martian Sludge Dossier, a big-time scandal sheet.

Conversation flowed easily. Slix Carragenaan, the reporter, asked Ralf a great many questions about Aronist artifacts, any possible resurgence of militancy among Covenant of the Sons of Aron sects, government cover-ups, and just exactly who he was and what Ralf was doing aboard the STARSLAMMER.

Ralf answered the questions politely and succinctly, carefully alternating the phrases 'no comment' and 'no statement will be issued at this time' so as not to repeat himself.

Chapter 5. The Farce Awakens

F ive hours after Knuckles's briefing, Ralf and his team entered the secure cargo deck aboard Space City C-0004 and finally faced the artifact.

"The basic design of the time vault, as this object might aptly be labelled, is that of early Rectilinear Blues, just post New-Wave Masonics. As we can see by the Rocanthiar fluted pillar work on the edges, and the heavily Northern-influenced Boberman lattice system, the design was originally and fundamentally a technologically utilitarian but quasi-formic dysfunctional representation of-"

"Looks like a big box to me," stated Haisenbreyer, cutting off Clokene's thoroughly informed yet impenetrably obscure monologue.

"Rectilinear would seem a strongly cogent appellation," mused Clokene agreeably.

"I wonder what's inside?" wondered Ralf, always the one to ask the most inappropriate question.

"That," spake Clokene, raising her finger as if it were a hypodermic about to inject a series of thoughts into Ralf, "is more of a recreational conversation curiosity than a serious interrogative. Surely you realize the purview of our mission is simply to act as couriers, not investigators into antiquarian Aronist matters."

"We're not allowed to open it?" suggested Ralf with the look of a young student taking a shot at a lengthy Kduimlian translation.

"Most certainly not," she pronounced.

"Ah, come on... let us gander until the urge is sated. Let us not let this resplendent curiosity's unveiling be belated," taunted a voice from beside the artifact.

"I believe you have used the word 'gander' in an inappropriate manner," snobbed Clokene staring, superiority evident, at the man with faded denim-fabric pants, a t-shirt with the non-word 'Chevy' emblazoned on the front, and hand vaser (appropriately in hand), who was cutting a large hole in the side of the artifact.

"Anything for a rhyme," shrugged the man.

"There's no homophone for a gander couplet," argued Clokene.

By this time Haisenbreyer had returned from examining the posterior sector of the artifact.

"Who the Noraville is this?" shouted the Colonel.

Ralf's mind screamed ADEPT. It was definitely Adept.

"What brazen subterfuge, uh," Clokene began to search her mind for some more interesting words with which to impress the Colonel.

"I'm the Acme Artifact Repairman, and I've come to repair your artifact!" answered the man brightly as he pulled a stiff body from the artifact's interior.

They stared at the pale and inert body. A Martianoid male. Youngish, with long hair. Thin, yet not malnourished. His shirt colourfully proclaimed 'Aron REAL ZEAL World Tour'.

Adept pressed a small black box to the carcass' neck, and a blue aura briefly flashed around the body. Adept straightened with his hands on his hips. His back gave a little cracking sound. He yawned widely.

"You will be billed through the proper channels. Ciao." He took a step away from the body, added "Yo, Ralf", nodded, and dematerialized.

"A friend of yours!?" demanded Haisenbreyer.

Ralf shook his head, aware that he was lying for the first time since he had told Mrs. Blackheart that no, he hadn't poured the litre of dried Delaroug body-lint and Raspberry School-Aid into the private (and clearly marked 'No Unauthorized Use') facial tissue box on her desk.

"He addressed you 'Ralf'," insinuated Clokene.

"Mmm. Luckily he didn't mail me! I wouldn't have

gotten very far addressed 'Ralf' now would I?" rattled Ralf, hoping the punch line's drum roll and cymbal crash in his head would drown out his internal scream of panic.

Before more solid accusations could be loosed, the three were interrupted by the carcass propping itself up and asking if anyone knew the time, or could suggest a nearby deli that might be open.

=

The re-animated carcass from prehistory, blandly recorded as 'Jon Doe' in the Space City's medical records, and his time vault artifact were hastily relocated to a highly secure medical bay deep inside the annulus of Space City C-0004.

Haisenbreyer wrung his hands. Droplets of sweat fell onto the deck. He, Clokene, and Ralf were watching 'Jon' in his private ward through a one-way mirror wall.

"I don't understand," moaned Haisenbreyer, wringing his left hand with his right and achieving several more droplets of sweat, "What is he doing?!"

"That is obvious," countered Clokene. "He is utilizing the electrically amplified vibrations of thin wires strung tightly over a solid body to produce pleasing random tonalities."

"I can see that!" bluffed Haisenbreyer, now wringing his right hand with his left.

"I thought he was playing a song with that electrical guitar," said Ralf, standing slightly behind the other two facing the mirrored wall.

"That's no song!" said Haisenbreyer sharply.

Ralf crossed his arms over his chest. "Everybody's a critic."

"You don't understand," shivered Haisenbreyer.

In the ward, Jon was sitting with a black guitar on his lap. He fretted the six strings in complicated patterns. The sounds were electrically amplified by the

large cube-shaped device he had dragged from inside
the artifact. He stopped for a moment, then repeated
what he had been singing with a slightly faster and
more complex musical accompaniment:

well have you said
so long
to the trees
waved into
the passing breeze
who knows
how long
we will be
alone
we're looking to
maintain the peace
that's reason enough
we already
burnt the lease
so don't make it rough
just say goodbye
to the blue sky
cause we're leaving this world
to make the red world
our new home place
where on the third naked day
Jammy led the flower children
from wilderness to play-V
there he taught them ancient beautiful ways
the simple, the sublime,
the ungaudy
pixelation uncompromised
we grew and prospered
and Jammy said all that has passed
was not too shoddy
we bless them a song
and keep moving along...

"Nora," breathed Haisenbreyer. "That's from the

Third of the 7 Holy Albums of Aron!"

"Perhaps he's a prophet!" suggested Ralf sunnily.

Clokene looked shocked. Haisenbreyer began to wring the rest of his body, producing huge amounts of sweat that soon made the floor slippery.

They carefully escorted Ralf out of the observation room, down the aft corridor and into a games room. It took them less than ten minutes to convince him that the most productive way he could spend the remainder of their time aboard C-0004 was to vie for top score on 'Mangle-a-Rabbitt' with the top competitors AAA and FTG.

Chapter 6. Greetings Of The Draconians

Bob Trook, the Commodore of Space City C-0004, was extruding a particularly pungent-smelling shot of expression vapour via her tentacle end orifice for the translator input slot on her big big desk.

"Gentlebeings," greeted her electronic proxy voice, "please make yourselves comfortable."

She motioned Clokene and Haisenbreyer to two plush chairs and waited until they were settled. She did not seek to clarify if they were indeed comfortable.

"Where is the third member of your group, the one named..." Trook glanced at a data pod on her desk, "Ralf?"

"Ralf is presently occupied with research on methods and procedures pertinent to our mission," scammed Clokene.

"I smell, I mean, I see."

Trook considered Ralf's absence for a moment while her two guests considered the fact that interacting with Ejsaanons, especially the ones of superior rank who did most of the talking, posed a clearly traumatic olfactory experience.

"You have some news for us, Commodore?"

"Affirmative. A communication from the PLASMIC SURFER, the ship that is to take you to Aqua Posteri 8. Their ETA is approximately twelve hours from now. I trust you will make arrangements with cargo services unit to have your charge transferred to that ship."

"We shall make arrangements," agreed Haisenbreyer for the both of them, being more concerned with getting away from the Commodore's rich aroma than the precise timeline for their mission.

=

Jon was at it again, sounding pleasant random tonalities with his guitar and singing Aronist scripture:

tinge your days joyous
and tints your words painless
laughter to provide
the sound of happiness
never doubt
its uncanny
you can rely upon
these words of Jammy

Haisenbreyer and Clokene entered the ward room. Jon went into bopping a simple rhythm with a bass string, and snapping high chords on the upstroke, as he muttered phrases:

can you feel
real zeal
does it heal
real zeal

"Jon-"

bend and kneel
real zeal
clutch and seal
real zeal

"There are some-"

do you really feel
...the re-al zeeee-allllllll, sustained Jon.

"-questions..." Haisenbreyer's sentence trailed off.

Clokene, feeling a mite more assertive, stepped to where Jon's amplifying device was connected to the room's power source, and broke the connection. As the high chord died in a crunch of static, Jon continued to stare down at his instrument, suddenly uncommunicative. After a moment of quiet, his head bounced up.

"Decided to talk to me already?" he asked cheerfully.

Haisenbreyer stared at him intently.

"We have important questions."

"So do I."

154

"That's fine." Haisenbreyer motioned to Clokene, and she activated the audio recorder in her pocket. "First, why have you been singing Aronist scriptures ever since you, er, arrived?"

"Aronist scripture? What's that? What I sing I have sung since it was first written; it is what I have sung all my life."

"You are a religious man, then?" asked Haisenbreyer.

Jon shrugged. "What do you mean by religious?"

"Religious in the Aronist sense- have you faith in Aron?"

Jon looked down at his guitar for a long moment. "I suppose I have a fair amount of faith in Aron."

"I see. We have dated your artifact, and find that it was constructed at approximately the same era when Aron was alive. Had you anything to do with the early Aronist movement?"

"Oh, I feel I must ask a few questions of you, before I will be able to answer yours comfortably. You've a terrible advantage."

"An equitable arrangement," interjected Clokene.

Jon smiled. "Thank you. First of all, where am I, when am I?"

"This is the Space Patrol Craft STARSLAMMER, docked at Space City C-0004, orbiting the planet Terra, in the Sol system. The Solar Sol is 1969 S.R. that's Since Reset, which is the Great Reset, a cataclysmic solar storm that wiped all electronic data long ago, almost two millennia ago. This is my associate, intelligence analyst Clokene Daggr." Haisenbreyer indicated Clokene with one hand.

"Enchanted." Jon kissed her wrist.

"And I am Colonel Haisenbreyer."

Jon shook his hand and said "Most pleased to meet you. My name is Buck. Buck Rogers."

Chapter 7. Close Encounters of the Revanchist Kind

Captain Sbor suspected that her most recent orders had originated from an obscured source, that is to say, had been handed down through multiple levels of rank and through several layers of the Alliance's bureaucratic institutions in a manner which would fog and confuse anyone's guess as to just who had initially written them.

This, however, was quite safely within the norm of the workings of Space Corps, or Space Patrol, or the Bureau Of Transparency, or the Office for Acquisition of Supplementary Data Pods, or any other arm of the Alliance's ubiquitous bureaucratic tentacles.

The orders had passed through Commodore Trook's office, and arrived aboard Sbor's ship moments earlier. Now they rested on an ejected pink data pod, awaiting reading.

Sbor had spent her coffee break assembling a Crylewnian 'Homogeneously Stylistic' jigsaw puzzle of a Futsillous Whiteback Furworm crawling over a patch of frozen carbon dioxide atop the nose of an albino polar bear-wolf. Needless to say, Sbor returned from her coffee break much refreshed and ready to mete out justice to those deserving.

"New orders have arrived, ma'am," reminded Myelin.

Sbor nodded her best brisk 'I can answer your carefully structured sentence with a sloppy nod anytime I want to because I'm the Captain' nod, and settled herself back atop her command chair.

Her new orders read:

=

STARSLAMMER- Space Patrol Craft- 1969.047-

1904.33511#
TO: Captain Siso Sbor
FROM: General Mary Poncherelli
Immediately issue arrest warrant for Space Corps
Colonel Ralf. Charges at your discretion. Complete
orders soonest.

=

The orders were followed by the usual verification
codes, but a further explanation of the order's sparse
content was not present.

Sbor grunted malcontentedly.

It appeared that whatever mysterious force had
released Ralf from the Grand Theft Spacecraft charge
earlier had finally realized its error. This new order was
effectively a cancel for the previous release order.
Although it smelled clandestine, the new order did
deliver justice, and truly a justice that had been
subverted up until that point in time.

Sbor had Myelin open a frequency to the security
director aboard the C-0004.

"I've got an arrest warrant for a Space Corps
officer," Sbor informed the little video screen in front
of her command chair.

"Nnnnnnn. Which officer you say?" breathed the
black leather clad figure in the screen.

"The one called Ralf. He's a Colonel. He, um,
escaped while being held for Grand Theft Spacecraft."

"The game?"

"No, the crime! He's most dangerous." Then, for
emphasis, she added, "He's a Terran."

=

In the corridors of Beta Section within Space City
C-0004, a high-pitched siren wailed.

"Forward!" screamed Lieutenant Beryl Krem.
"Come on, you Rews! Git yer lower limbs into
motion!"

As the invading mass of Friggians pushed forward,

deeper into the interior of the huge Space City, bitter comments gurgled only softly among the lower ranks. Lieutenant Krem was a decorated leader, despite the fact that he kept to the extreme rear of his men, and drove them on with his handmade three-meter-long Belaznian-hide whip.

=

In the Control Centre of C-0004, Pob Trook was discovering what it feels like when your peptic ulcers come off in chunks and edge up your throat. C-0004 orbited Terra. How the Noraville was it being attacked by Friggians?

She summoned her security director and apprised him of the situation. He agreed to take immediate defensive action. She summoned her superiors on Mars. They agreed to send supplementary forces immediately. She summoned her wet masseuse. It agreed to renegotiate their contract, immediately.

In the middle of intense negotiation with her masseuse on the ever important 'Personal Time Leave Benefits' clause, Trook was interrupted by her communications officer. The battle between Alliance and Friggian forces in Beta Section had caused a large internal fire, she was informed.

Trook had been awarded the Electricity Conservation Award of 1967, and took this opportunity to further her intense interest in resource conservation and waste control by ordering her communications officer to see that all the 'No Smoking' signs in that Beta Section were turned off.

After that, Trook retired to her office to escape the constant lull of activity in her Control Centre.

Scant moments later, her intercom buzzed.

"Yes, what?"

"Commodore Trook, I have a Doctor Mahad to see you," said the intercom.

"I told you I wanted all my appointments for today

cancelled!" snapped Trook.

"But he doesn't have an appointment, ma'am."

"Oh, okay. Send him in."

The bespectacled doctor shuffled in. As soon as Trook saw him, she knew he was an Ihnewian. He had the one unmistakable trait of the Ihnewians: his upper eyelashes curved downwards as drastically as his lower lashes curved upwards. This caused an interesting phenomenon: every time he blinked, his eyelids locked together. To re-open his eyes he had to twitch his eyebrows in a much exaggerated manner. The result of all this was that, to the untrained observer, and most lounge comedians, Ihnewians all looked as if they had a severe facial tic.

The doctor was the first to speak. "I must talk vit you, Commodore!"

"What is it, Doctor, er, uh, Mahad?" The name rang some deep alarm bell in Trook's third auxiliary digestion vestibule.

"I have invented some ting vitch will eradicate ze terrible Friggians from zis City!"

The Commodore considered his accent, then asked "Really? What is it?"

Doctor Mahad paused for a moment, hoping to create a dramatic effect. He leaned over Trook's desk and said, as slowly as possible, "Mechanized... carnivorous... celery!"

"Oh, how nice," said Trook nicely, as she reached for the nice little button on the side of her nice little desk that would bring the nice not-so-little men in their nice little white suits. Hopefully, these nice men would be nice enough to bring along their nice little straight jackets and some intravenous relaxants.

"Nice?!" screamed Doctor Mahad madly. "Zis invention could be the one weapon to destroy the Friggian Federation! Vat's that little button you just pushed?"

"Oh, this nice little button?" asked Trook nicely.

Dr. Mahad spun around and made for the door. He was mad, but he wasn't stupid.

"Vit or vit out your help, my killer celery vill destroy the Friggians! You haven't seen the last of Doctor Maaaa-haaaaaaadddddddd!" screamed the Ihnewian as he ran down the corridor.

Chapter 8. Detention, Deflection, and Destruction

R alf never made it to the Control Centre. He reached corridor X-1138, and that was it. The forces of justice were too mighty to allow him to reach the Control Centre where who knows what havoc he might wreak.

"You Ralf?" grunted the security officer, shoving his index finger with a directional gesture at Ralf, and actually doing a fair Rip impersonation.

"Me Ralf!" Ralf agreed readily, jabbing his thumb at his own chest, and nodding his head sharply. An early brain-load had made Ralf understand that it is always best to mimic the style of your opposite in any communication.

The security officer looked at Ralf for a moment, not sure whether he should smile at the joke that was somehow intertwined in their conversation thus far, or bash in his head.

Ralf's intensely serious look cracked, and Ralf smiled slightly in embarrassment.

"You under arrest."

"What?" Ralf took a step back from the officer.

"Arrest. You. Under. Okay?" grunted the officer, as he pulled out his black neutron-metal handcuffs.

Ralf took another step back.

"Come."

He began to reach for Ralf, who took another step back, then two more, then several more.

"Stop!" The security officer took two steps, lifted Ralf off his feet, and slapped the cuffs around his wrists.

"You can't arrest me! What for!?" shrieked Ralf.

The officer thought for a moment.

"Resisting arrest."

=

Around this same time, both Clokene and Haisenbreyer were wishing for a bit of protective custody. After completing their first interview with Buck Rogers, they found their route to the Control Centre blocked by information-hungry media people.

Their path now led through a no martianoid's land of overhead microphone booms, shiny video cameras, and rabid, snapping news interrogators.

"Can you tell us, is the artifact a remnant of a superior civilization, predating our own?" The Martian Daily.

"Is it true, does the artifact contain newly discovered Aronist scriptures? Have you uncovered a sacred cache of forgotten enlightenment?" Alliance Datasheet.

"How can you deny this, the artifact is actually an inoperative spaceship scouting in preparation of an extra-dimensional invasion, and the invaders look like deformed Kduimlians!" Martian Sludge Dossier.

"No comment, no comment, and how can you tell if a Kduimlian is deformed?" shot back Haisenbreyer, covering all bases at once.

But before Haisenbreyer even finished his statement, another barrage of questions spewed forth.

"Let me handle this." Clokene elbowed in front of Haisenbreyer. "Gentlebeings, any statement we might issue pertaining to our current situation will be riddled with the imprecision of inadequate research, and darkened by the shadow of expertise forced into a novel battle of the intellect see-sawing between uncertainties and under the conditions of an exigent state of affairs. Our purpose is neither that of ascertaining original data, nor of communicating these to public media services. With the same fairness and passion for the truth which drives you, the mouthpieces of cultural and social

162

forces, to seek out and interpret elements of change, or 'news', within your milieu, notwithstanding the motivation of eventual assimilation vis a vis these elements into an improved society, I find I must remain in guarded posture. No other reaction on my part can be acceptable to myself, or any other public servant with the same moral values, precognitive behavioural tendencies, or sense of duty to any real or conceived benevolent authority structure."

Already the crowd had begun to disperse.

Some muttered "Okay okay, all right then, just say no comment why don't you?"

Haisenbreyer smiled at Clokene with the look of a psychopath realizing that a hammer destroys with at least as much ease at it creates. Clokene didn't smile back, maybe because she realized that it was her hammer.

=

Commodore's Log 1969.051-0900   Commodore Pob Trook recording:
C-0004 declared Emergency Status at <1969-051.0710>.

At that time three Friggian Battle Skimmers were spotted at (coordinates redacted). Boarding began minutes after the initial alert. As all three ships are maintaining random velocity and direction, it has been impossible to confront them directly. It is estimated approximately three hundred Friggian soldiers are now operating in C-0004's Beta Section.

Our security forces were immediately mobilized and have succeeded in containing the invasion to Beta Section so far. This detente is unlikely to last indefinitely as an uncontrolled fire caused by the altercation is now, after destroying most of Beta Section, destroying some bulkheads leading to Delta Section which contains the City's menagerie.

Due to the predatory nature of many of the beasts

there contained, other sections of the City may soon become populated with 'predators', be they Friggian or animal. This might place our forces in a position where retreat is unavoidable.

=

While Commodore Trook sat in her private office relaying the day's events into the permanent log, the crises continued in the Control Centre.

"Sub-Commodore! The fire has broken through to Delta Section!" screamed a technician.

"Technician! Many thanks for explaining the obvious!" loudly translated the command speaker after Sub-Commodore Klick Hipdip twitched its antennae, and made a series of clicking noises by repeatedly striking its thorax with both prothoracic legs.

The Technician pouted. "Well, what are we gonna do now? All those narsty creatures overrunning the ship! How can we hope to survive?"

Sub-Commodore Hipdip flexed cryptically as it slipped an fresh data pod from under its desk and initiated a requisition for several gross of Pooper Scoopers.

Chapter 9. A Canticle for Euhemerists

The small diplomatic shuttle BOOGIETUBES rested in the magnetic docking clamp embrace of Space City C-0004. BOOGIETUBES had been commissioned by the Department of Acquisition for the Chamber of Arbitrary Social Justice for the purpose of delivering a replacement for the arrested and now incarcerated Space Corps Officer Ralf who had been part of the entourage travelling to Aqua Posteri 8.

Ralf's replacement was none other than the Martian who had originally briefed Ralf on that assignment. Knuckles had come to handle the mission personally.

Knuckles wasted no time. From his point of boarding the City he strode directly to the Control Centre. He was immediately allocated a state room where he quickly shaved, showered, trimmed his toenails, carefully examined a burgeoning wart, and practised his trombone for half an hour.

From there, he moved swiftly to the Recreation Area where he dashed through the formalities of playing a set of zero-gee basketball with each of the City's major political figures. After that, another shower was necessary.

Life is full, Knuckles thought to himself.

He then dropped his laundry off at Speedy's Sludge Removal & Laundry Care before nipping around to interrogate the mysterious figure from ancient times.

=

Haisenbreyer and Clokene had been summoned there by Knuckles, but they arrived at the anteroom to Buck Roger's secure chamber first.

On Knuckles's pre-arrival orders, Buck's room itself had been stripped of all artifacts. The anteroom however had been converted to a miniature museum with ancient books, sheet music, musical instruments and equipment, drug paraphernalia, various clothing items, bizarre seemingly non-functional doodads and gizmos, plus various unidentifiable knickknacks.

Knuckles held one ancient object in his hand. An extremely squat grey cylinder. "So, what is it?"

"An initial inspection revealed the contents to be a thin strip of plastic, on which innumerable minuscule sequential photographic negatives have been chemically induced. Research performed by media scientists in the City, acting on an original premise of mine, have found it to be a primitive form of motion picture." Clokene mouthed the archaic phrase with nostalgic enthusiasm. "The audio track was found to be co-located alongside the visual images and was our method of discovering the proper viewing speed for the antiquated media."

Knuckles turned to Haisenbreyer. "So, what is it?"

"Video of Buck Rogers in his own time. We've seen bits of it when they were trying to figure out the right speed, but not the whole thing. Our mission is to be couriers, not investigative historians. The lab did, however, rig up a device to view the cylinder."

Haisenbreyer nodded toward the jury-rigged device on the table.

"Does it work?"

"Probably," shrugged Haisenbreyer.

Knuckles handed him the cylinder.

"Put it on."

Haisenbreyer handed Clokene the cylinder. Clokene looked questioningly back at Knuckles.

"Consider yourself an investigative historian. Put it on."

Clokene removed the reel from the cylinder, threaded the leading end of the strip into the device, and initiated playback.

The screen showed whiteness flickering, then blackness. Then a grey circle enclosing the number ten.

A second-hand-like arm swept fully around once, and then it read nine. Then eight. Then seven. All the way down to one. The screen was blank for a moment; the soundtrack blipped, and it began.

"Tonight! Hard Core Broadcasting with FM 99.8 brings you a show we like to call "Aron live"! Carefully manipulated editing brings you twenty minutes of outrageous concert footage that appears unedited! For this and other subliminally truthful statements of non-importance, your favourite Master of Ceremonies, Mole Swineback!!"

Cut to a close-up of a bright pink pig wearing a cowboy hat. The subtitles whipped by the bottom of the screen incredibly fast. They read: "Oink, oink, snort, snuffle, oink, squeal, snort..."

The soundtrack then emits a glib intro by a weathered broadcaster: "Got a really big shew for you tonight."

Cut to a huge auditorium packed with martianoids. The audience roars intoxicated enthusiasm. The main event is obviously about to begin. The view switches through an assortment of five different angles, watching Buck Rogers and three other martianoids cross the grand stage and strap on, climb into, or sit in front of their instruments.

Strange music swells to life. Buck sings as he plays a musical device closely resembling the one recovered from the artifact:

Earthlings, dirtlings
don't be hurt things
we love you all
and your dirty wings
Jammy was divine,
the god of rhythm and rhyme
lifted our ears and hearts
to heaven and even beyond
gifted us truth and beauty

167

unless you have been conned
don't trust anyone
over thirty minutes away
they won't be here in time
and cannot empathize
all we can do is rise rise rise
ever higher
our red eyes the wiser

The three investigative historians watched in mute, open-mouthed disbelief.

Chapter 10. Axiom Me Later

Ralf was on the verge of anger. He felt that his unexpected imprisonment was some form of back stab devised by those same forces which had brought him to C-0004 in the first place. He had sat staring at the blank wall of his cell for about an hour, and, yes, he was definitely on the verge of anger. One more thing would very likely burst the dam of pent-up petulance.

At the last possible moment, he was spared the ravages of that powerful emotion by a kindness from his two guards. They ventured into conversation with him.

"Are you really a Terran?" asked the younger of the two.

Ralf nodded without enthusiasm.

"We don't see too many of you people up here. See, no third eye?" the younger guard prodded the older, who merely grunted a mild interest.

"What's the difference anyway between Terran and Martian? I mean, we look alike, and both believe in Aron, right?"

"That's true," agreed Ralf. "They're both beautiful planets."

"But you guys have some additional beliefs, a different sacred discography?"

"Well," Ralf was reluctant to get into religious talk. "We do have the Three Axioms of Aron."

"I've heard of that somewhere, but what were they, these Axioms?" asked the second guard, obviously intelligent but perhaps not very well-read.

"There were three," said Ralf.

"Yeah. I know that. So what's the first?" the younger guard butted in.

"No one knows, and what is more, no one cares," recited Ralf.

169

"That's not a very positive attitude," argued the older guard.

"If it works, don't fix it," added Ralf.

"The attitude may work, but it doesn't sound very healthy," countered the younger guard.

"On even the longest journey, the first step is always quite near your left foot," continued Ralf.

"Is that the first Axiom?" asked the younger guard.

"No." Ralf looked surprised. "That's the third."

"Well what's the first?"

"No one knows, and what is more-"

"Aww, don't say that, dude" protested the younger guard.

"You asked me to say that!!" Ralf's frustration was finally clear in his voice.

"What? Is the third the only important Axiom? Are the others of lesser importance?"

"They are equal," explained Ralf.

"Why not name another one for us, then?"

"I am trying!" protested Ralf.

"It's not working! We only know the one!" The guard was getting upset. He raised a finger at Ralf, presumably to demonstrate the number of Axioms he had as of present learned. "Try something else!"

"If it works, don't fix it," recited Ralf again.

"But it's not working!"

"Tell us the first," pleaded the older guard.

"No one knows, and what is more, no one cares."

"That's not true! You know-" the older guard pointed to Ralf, "-and I care!"

The heated debate was cut short when an urgent communication beeped on the guard console just outside Ralf's cell. The younger guard stepped out to check the audio message.

Moments later, he was back in the cell, eyes wild, hair standing aloft in shock, his capacity for believing the unsuspected unexpectedly enlarged.

"The celery are coming!!" he shrieked.

Chapter 11. The Stainless Steel Celery

Theta Section of C-0004 was in the throes of panicked evacuation. On the port side, Friggians battled fiercely, killing innocent citizens of the City, looting their homes, burning their business places, buying their soft drinks in recyclable bottles and paying the price net of deposit, all the while not planning to return the empties.

The Friggians fought with ferocious fervour for many reasons: political fanaticism, training in the blitzkrieg method of war, and not least, a wish to outrun the smoke and flames of the roaring conflagration their pillaging had started in the sections already visited.

On the starboard side of Theta Section, the celery were on the rampage. The insidious deadly green stalks roamed the corridors and thoroughfares, snatching martianoids and other citizens at random, and chewing them into pulpy, stringy masses. Ironically enough, the sound of a martianoid being chewed by celery is much the same as the sound produced by celery being chewed by a martianoid.

Chapter 12. Genesis of Exegesis

The bizarre cinematic premiere occurring in Buck Roger's antechamber continued.

On the screen, Buck sat slouched on a very wide chair, perhaps long enough to seat three people. To one side of him, a grinning male martianoid sat behind a desk. The view zoomed in to a two-shot of the pair.

"You found the clip somewhat distressing?"

"Yeah, most," shrugged Buck. "The thing of it is, I find that type of band very offensive. They purport to be anti-religious, at least that's how their fans see them, but they're not anti-religious at all. They're just as religious as The Thomas Goode Old-Time Bible Thump, or Candid Gospel Camera, or the Hallelujah Hour. They are religious; they're just perversely religious."

"And that's where Aron comes in?"

Buck nodded. "A constructive counter-movement to the forces that spawned Satan's Platelets, The Walking Willful, and the ultimate unlistenable perversion of our morality instinct, the four idiots who call themselves Mean Gods." Buck turned to look directly at the camera. "Yes folks, proof positive, the Forces of Evil can crush souls, and ladle out despair, but they cannot correctly tune a low B string!"

Before further accusations on Buck's part could occur, a large black note pushed the frame containing Buck and his interviewer up and out of view. The note was followed by a parade of other similar notes. Lines formed, and soon the camera was zipping along a musical staff populated by clusters of notes. The music cross-fades into ambient crowd noise as the notated staff morphs to a small, crowded nightclub where Buck and associates again perform on stage.

Buck sings:

I'm a voodoo child
but it ain't too wild
being reviled
while yer here
defiled when yer gone
not what I want
not my idea of self-styled
I move hearts and hands
with runs and spans
cosmic sense-bending tricks
with the fixed one thru six
the course sets the plans
you know
while I net my kicks
yeah, I'll show...

The phrase 'Esus Jam (The Newest Of All)' crawled across the bottom of the screen as Buck began to manipulate his guitar at an incredible speed. The entire next three minutes of the film were devoted to various close-ups and medium shots of Buck's instrumental wizardry. Finally, he sustained an E-flat suspended fourth chord for more than five seconds before singing again, now while strumming in free time:

the best thing
you can do
to divinity
is stretch out
your silver grasp
and pull it down
from infinity

Clokene chortled snobbishly during one extreme close-up, turning the others' attention momentarily away from the video. Knuckles and Haisenbreyer eyed her questioningly.

"Soft focus and a jump shot," she critiqued with a snotty wave of her hand.

Chapter 13. Deus Ex Machina

Theta Section was almost entirely overwhelmed by the carnivorous celery. Among the last few survivors to flee the doomed section were Ralf and his two guards. The three moved through silent corridors without exchanging a word.

"Trade a 'yo' for a 'hey'?" Ralf asked the older guard.

"I'd rather not, under the circumstances."

Just as they stepped into a lift car (which differs from an auto-lift car solely by having higher quality muzak), a figure dressed in the uniform of the Space City sanitation department leapt forward, grabbed each of the guards by their furthest back, left molars, and flung them out of the lift car.

The stranger hopped inside, and the lift car doors snapped rudely shut.

"Holy Aron!!" Ralf shouted in surprise. "Why'd you do that?"

"I dunno. It just seemed the beauty way to go," smirked the stranger.

"No way." Ralf shook his head.

"Yes way." The stranger nodded.

"But who are you?"

Before the stranger could answer, their lift car stopped and its doors opened. The mysterious stranger strode out. Ralf tagged along, half running to keep up to the vigorous stride of his rescuer. They turned down an obscure and vacant corridor, where the stranger abruptly stopped.

"You know me." The stranger smiled.

It took Ralf a few seconds. No beard? Then: "Captain Berishu!" Up came Ralf's most proper salute.

"Cut the militaristic bourgeois crap," rumbled the Captain. His vigorous stride cut in again, and Ralf scampered along beside him.

"But you died! You got sucked out the airlock on the NOSFERATU because of that crazy Quelfin!"

The Captain stopped abruptly again, causing Ralf to slightly overshoot his position, and then retreat to it hastily. "Ralf," the Captain said intently.

"Yes?" Ralf's eyes darted about nervously.

"There's something important you must do. I don't want you to do it for me. I don't want you to do it for the Alliance. I want you to do it for you!"

"Is it hard?"

"It is a matter of life and death for millions of people. It will place great responsibility on you, a responsibility that others may try to usurp. It may even cost you your life, or at the very least, several weekends."

"Sounds hard," hedged Ralf.

"Ralf..." Again, that intensity. "Are you looking for purpose in your life?"

"Mmm. Not really."

"My Aron, Ralf, do you not feel a passion for purpose in this meaningless maze of foolish contests we call our lives?"

"What for?" asked Ralf.

Berishu grabbed him by the shoulders, "Exactly. Now you've got it! That's the spirit!!" And back to his vigorous stride.

They turned onto a busier corridor. People hustled up one end and other people down the other.

"Hi there, soldier." A tightly clothed woman breathed hot words onto Ralf.

Ralf smiled at the woman as he unconsciously fingered the military insignia on his Space Corps form-fits, but continued scampering, still mostly focused on Berishu.

"The airlock! What about the airlock? And crazy Quelfin?"

"What about them?"

"You died!"

"No I didn't."

"You did! You died in Part I!"

Berishu stopped abruptly. "Well, if you're gonna get technical. Let's look at The Book."

Berishu grabbed a loosely bound sheaf of papers from a shocked looking scholarly type (yes, black-rimmed glasses) who had been travelling the opposite direction.

"Let's see..." Berishu licked his thumb, an unfortunate habit, and flipped through the front part of the manuscript. "Book 1... Book 2... back a little ways..."

"What are you doing?!" shrieked the scholarly type.

"Hang onto your hangnails. Just looking something up."

"You can't do that!! You're not supposed to read that- especially not here!" The manuscript's owner looked nervously about the corridor. Berishu ignored him.

"Right here, Ralf." Berishu tapped the page with his finger. "Says: 'then he felt a tremendous movement of air, and the coldness of the void touched him.' Nice line. Almost poetic, but nothing about death! Nothing about me flying out of the airlock and bursting like an organ-filled balloon-bat on Orchtus 4!"

"I don't understand..."

"Quelfin was an idiot! He forced me into the airlock and then turned the air conditioning on full blast. I had a cold for weeks afterward. The sneezing, the coughing, maybe being sucked out into space would have been less traumatic!"

"That's what this means?" Ralf's forehead creased and he shook his head at the manuscript. "Coldness of the void? Air conditioning?!"

Berishu handed the manuscript back to the scholarly

type who just averted his eyes, blushed, and backed slowly away into the shadows.

Chapter 14. Martian Time-Blip

Buck Rogers clutched his sides as peals of phlegm-scraping laughter forced a way through up his torso and out his throat. He fell off his chair with a thump.

The interviewer squirmed uncomfortably. This was the first time he had received a reaction like this to a deep (deep for an entertainment interview anyway) question.

"Terry... Terry?" the interviewer called to Buck on the floor. "We're glad you're happy to be on our show..." Buck continued to laugh, and the interviewer looked directly at the camera. "It's nice to see a guest enjoying himself answering my questions."

Buck looked up from his prostrate position. "I'm sorry. That question always gets me."

The interviewer shrugged. "Who created the world? A rather obvious question to ask someone like you, someone who claims no religious belief, and yet writes songs seen by your fans as not only religious but, apostolic, for lack of a better word."

"Well, obvious question, but the assumptions inherent in the question, not so obvious. I could answer your question 'mu', but I am not a grazing cow. So I will answer your question more directly."

Buck turned to gaze into the lens and affects the host's voice:

"'Who created the world' you ask?" Buck's eyes smiled, and he revealed his teeth. "We are..!"

The frame cut to a close up of an adult martianoid with a trumpet. He blew one triumphant note.

Next, fireworks exploded astride a starry sky as the congregated multitude released a crowd of balloons.

A marching band stopped mid-step, and leapt into the air to click their heels.

Buck, sweaty and shirtless but wearing his same guitar, moved towards the back of a grand stage where a long line of two-meter tall letters spelled 'Jammy Handtrickes' and did a karate kick, flattening the letter 'e'. He then tugged at one guitar tuning peg and his instrument growled into a yet lower register.

Concert-goers broke through the barricades and rushed Aron on stage.

Cut to a band of elephants storming the streets of a small dusty town.

Then an entourage of several automobiles drove leisurely down a deep, narrow passage between urban architectural behemoths as hundreds of kilograms of paper confetti rained down.

A herd of white buffalo bolted over a cliff in a frenzied abandonment of the law of gravity.

A long shot of Terra began to zoom in as a well-sustained but distorted guitar chord (Ebsus4 to be specific) began to swell in volume. It ended abruptly as the zoom-in reached a cloud layer and the frame turned white.

The end of the plastic video strip flapped harmlessly against the little contraption that continued to spin its reel. The film had ended.

"Not quite your average Movie of the Week," noted Haisenbreyer.

"Far from modal, indeed," agreed Clokene calmly.

Knuckles turned to them with fiery intensity. "Don't you understand what this means?"

"Not especially. Maybe you better fill us in," invited Haisenbreyer.

"Him!" Knuckles pointed at the sealed door beside the wall they had projected the video on. "He's not 'Buck Rogers'! He's not an ancient Aronist priest! He comes from Nora with this!" Knuckles snatched the plastic reel in one hand and held it aloft, "This monstrosity! This religious atrocity, this blasphemy. He is the Nora, and his coming signifies the beginning of the Final Weekend of Ugly Judgments and Just Beautiful Irony! He must be destroyed if we are to survive! His existence must be utterly expelled, his will crushed, and his guitar strings cut! There can be no argument. There is no room for pity or charity in what must be our immediate and swift dealing with this insult to the grace of Aron! Do you understand?"

"Quite," acknowledged Clokene. "But should we not listen to what Buck has to say before we leap to any conclusions?"

"Leap to conclusions? I am a reasonable person. I will listen to rational arguments." Knuckles shrugged. "I would not be one to condemn others in ignorance. Such a thing is not fitting for a citizen of my learning. Let us allow the viperous beast to tempt us with his slick words of damnation before we destroy him."

"Go team!" cheered Haisenbreyer, somewhat wanly.

The three moved into the inner chamber, and found Buck fingering his guitar, as usual.

"Hey gang! What's happening in the 25th century today?" grinned Buck.

"Buck," Clokene began.

"Don't call it that!" shrieked Knuckles. "Just another deception from the tempter!"

"Oh, is something wrong?" questioned Buck, looking back and forth between the three somewhat obsequiously.

"We saw the video."

"Ah."

"I think an explanation is called for," understated Clokene.

"Reveal your woeful treachery, Hideous Nora!" snarled Knuckles.

"Nora? That's not my name!"

"Go ahead!" urged Knuckles nastily.

"What?"

"Go ahead and tell us your name. Tell us you are Aron! See? We have guessed your deceptions before they have even passed your lips!"

"I'm not Aron, per se. I'm one part of Aron. Its songwriter and guitarist. Aron is my musical group. My name is Terry Aaronstrum- Aron takes its name from mine."

"You would tell us that Aronism arose from your simpleminded musical works! A trans-galactic system of belief and morality is nothing but the transmogrification and extension of your music?" questioned Clokene.

Aaronstrum looked admiringly at Clokene. "This Aronism you speak of sounds more like my last release, the Jammy Handtrickes' Electric Church," smiled he.

"No." Knuckles shook his head. "You dare invoke the name of our messiah? Next thing you'll be telling us the healing vibration of the Esus is fiction as well! You deal in despair, you clangorous abomination. You would reduce the wisdom of our religion from cosmic revelation to stray rhyming lines!"

"Now that's not logical!" Aaronstrum wagged a finger at them, and then gently strummed an E-flat sus4 chord, letting it sustain and ring in the air. "Beauty is beauty. Wisdom is wisdom. What difference does it make if the origin is from Earth, or beyond? Does that change its value?"

"Earth?" howled Knuckles incredulously. "Aronism began on Terra? On the third planet??"

Aaronstrum nodded. "South Saskatchewan, to be exact."

"Did you say Scratch & Win?" sought Clokene.

"They're right! They were right all along!!" shouted Knuckles.

"Who?" Aaronstrum reacted to Knuckles's vagueness.

"The Covenant of the Sons of Aron! They believed

that Martiankind originated on Terra! That Aronism began there! And that, therefore, Terra is the chosen planet, and Terrans the chosen people!"

Terry raised an eyebrow at Knuckles. "You're pretty sick, y'know?"

The air crackled, and the martianoid formerly identified as the Acme Artifact Repair Man popped into existence at Aaronstrum's side. He touched the musician's shoulder, and twisted a dial on the device hanging from his belt. Both beings disappeared through a puff of instantaneous transwarp transfer turbulence.

"No!" wailed Knuckles. "We could've destroyed him!"

"I thought we were to consider ourselves investigative historians, not vengeance seekers for Aronist dogma."

"Clokene, Clokene. So naive in matters of the spirit," patronized Knuckles, "You don't understand what's going on here."

"Okay," agreed Clokene. "If, as my superior officer, that is your opinion, via the McBeerson Act, Article four, Section three, I hereby remove myself from active duty until I can be relocated to a post more suited to your view of my abilities, at the same pay."

Clokene used the door.

Knuckles stared after her in wonder. Finally, he looked back to Haisenbreyer and shrugged dismissively.

"Know-it-all."

Chapter 15. Terralight

Clokene returned to her temporary quarters in Alpha Section and began analyzing the ancient documents found within the time capsule. The stasis chamber was a multi-fold. It contained several chambers, each apparently filled during a different time period.

One chamber, the oldest, contained the martianoid now identifying himself as Terry Aaronstrum, and some artifacts related to his unimaginably ancient time period.

Another chamber yielded documents younger, but still dated from long before the Great Reset, perhaps five thousand sols ago. The translator indicated that the written script was an archaic version of Old Low Terran. Clokene's eyes raced over the material, absorbing a new view of history that had long lay obscured by the dust of time.

Terry's band 'Aron' had been wildly successful in its day, a very strange and counter-intuitive time when Terra was the only known life-sustaining planet.

There were severe problems with the existing, major religions of the planet at that time. The different faiths had each evolved and offered a philosophy based on universal love and brotherhood. However, small differences among the variants of the religious tenets had either directly caused or exacerbated countless battles and wars between nation-states. By Terry's time, the world was in ruins, and the survivors were looking for a new banner under which to coalesce.

After so much devastating upheaval and conflict, the regular forces of legal and religious sanction were jettisoned. The desire for beauty and the enjoyment of life became paramount.

Instead of focusing on goodness and purity, the new

184

mystics focused on beauty, promising it after death. Action and prejudice were viewed as reckless, but passive prejudgment and aesthetic contemplation were viewed as holy. Beauty in life would be achieved through the joy of harmony and peace.

Aron's public image fit well with this new perspective of the highest societal value as beauty, not righteousness. Results, not efforts were commended. Beauty was the absolute, and its precursors and criteria were joy and harmony.

This new philosophy, based on the creation and appreciation of beauty, sprang forth based mostly on the lyrics of Terry's musical group and an urgent desire for a new beginning after some unspecified cataclysm. The martianistic (or 'humanistic' in the Terran phraseology) duty of every citizen was to create beauty in the world, to nurture beauty, and to appreciate what beauty spontaneously existed.

The final release from Aron was an extended satirical ensemble music piece titled 'Jammy Handtrickes Electric Church' which appeared to discuss a prophet or messiah for the god Aron, all the while possibly being a satire of the current ruling powers, or so some of the included media reviews claimed.

The humour was unrecognizable, and clearly the actual players were lost to history, thought Clokene.

In the satire, Jammy was the Son of Aron who came to Earth (or Terra, as the Martians prefer to call it) only to be literally drowned by political forces not ready for his message. His music, being divine, had the power to heal and to bring all enlightened beings together. His return would be announced by a great harmonious sound that would bring all spirit together and was known as the Esus.

The cover of this grand final work was simply the Aronist equation:

from which the primary icon of Aronism, the Equal Sign, or '=', no doubt originated.

People seemed to believe that this music, which had apparently been painstakingly recovered and re-created from similar works of an artist in an even earlier era, was a powerful tool for accessing the metaphysical, and a profound revelation for the ages.

As the new philosophy of Aronism took hold, prosperity returned and the inhabitants of Terra began to transform an uninhabitable nearby planet into a new colony. Thus Mars was born.

Clokene did not even pause to absorb all these startling revelations. She realized her time with these unique relics could be cut short at any moment. Once Knuckles realized what type of world-inverting information had been uncovered, it would no doubt be immediately suppressed.

So Clokene pushed on.

The translator had less difficulty with a second set of documents which dated to just before the time of the Great Reset. Here the Old Low Terran was more standard, and indeed some cross-fertilization with ancient Martian fonts was evident.

Almost two thousand sols ago, Aronism had spread across two worlds, Terra and Mars. But it was not a unifying phenomenon.

The variant of Aronism that thrived on Terra was based on the idea that the creation of beauty was the duty of the courageous. An active role was required of every person. Metaphysics were irrelevant to this variant. Aronism was more a philosophy, or technique for meaningful living. Aron was viewed as a prophet, but not divine.

In contrast, the Martian variant of Aronism viewed the existence of beauty as divine, not martian. The sole and supreme deity, Aron, demanded that all citizens appreciate the beauty of the cosmos, as provided by this ethereal god for their benefit. The notion of cosmic justice wormed its way back into the new belief system: those who had endured an unlovely life would be rewarded with beauty in the afterlife.

The two divergent views caused friction between Terra and its now thriving colony. Soon, Mars threatened to secede from the Terran political system. Things got unlovely. Ultimatums were delivered and ignored. An attack was launched. A war resulted.

When the fog and fire of combat had passed, both civilizations were devastated. Interplanetary travel was no longer possible due to the economic and political turmoil. Each planet would have to survive independently.

The document ended with an exhortation to see the beauty in diversity, including in one's enemies. Obviously the person writing the final section of the document had not been part of the power structure that had dictated events reach this ultimate low point.

The capsule had been buried on a near-Terra asteroid and forgotten, while the remnants of Terran civilization faltered on the cusp of extinction.

Clokene's knowledge of early history filled in the blanks. A few hundred sols after the forgotten Terra-Mars war, the Great Reset had occurred. A great economic and political collapse ensued after giant sunspots erupted on the surface of Sol. Coronal mass ejections followed which wiped out all the electronic data-nets on which both civilizations depended. Only some printed books and vinyl recordings survived.

Hundred of sols of painful knowledge reconstruction followed. Much of the ancient technology was reclaimed, but history remained obscure.

When Martians finally returned to Terra, they found

a tiny population of martianoids that they believed to be an ancient, long forgotten and abandoned Martian colony. Re-colonization followed, and the folk tales from Terra of a great lost civilization were dismissed as myth.

Clokene finished her notes, careful to add qualifiers to all her assertions. She had provided a complete rewrite of the history of the founding planet of the Alliance which upended all conventional thought, but this was just her interpretation. It was preliminary. It was tentative. It required a convergence of opinion. She welcomed input. It was not her fault.

Clokene did a final spellcheck, and sent her report to Knuckles.

Chapter 16. Thunderwords Are No

When Knuckles reviewed his messages, he immediately read Clokene's report in its entirety. It was rather long and, although he tried to stop and move on to other urgent matters at several points, he found he could not. The content was riveting, fascinating, and completely unacceptable.

Knuckles ordered a BOTCH Most Secret classification for Clokene's document. No other eyes would review this material until the Chamber For Arbitrary Social Justice had a chance to hear BOTCH's arguments on why it should be buried forever.

Later, Knuckles had a religious/spiritual experience in his private quarters, or possibly a stroke.

=

Improbably, Ralf was also having a mystical visitation at the precise same moment as Knuckles. Not the same mystical visitation necessarily, but a simultaneous and similar one nonetheless.

Ralf and Berishu had returned to Berishu's current home, a four-meter-wide square crate located in a secondary cargo bay of the space city. Berishu had customized the crate to the best of his abilities. He had draped tapestries on the inner sides, installed cable video, side to side carpeting, and an eight-speed blender. Despite all this, resale value on the dwelling remained quite low. This disturbed Berishu only occasionally.

Berishu's sleep/wake cycle was such that Shift 2 aboard the Space City was night. It was Shift 2. Berishu slept.

Ralf had crashed on the violet chaise set beside the entrance to the crate, but had awoken after only one cramp-inducing hour of sleep. He wandered around outside the crate, amid the jungle of such crates populating the cargo bay. It was there, next to a crate containing three gross of quarter-centimeter machine micro-screws that Ralf had his experience.

One moment, he stood calmly, contemplating the squeaking sounds his brandless sneakers could make on the smooth floor, and the next moment, an un-martian-like voice called to him from beyond.

First ethereally soft, then dramatically louder.

"Raaaaaaalf... Raaaaaaaaalf... er, RALF!!"

Ralf quit squeaking his shoes.

"Ralf, yo, whazzup?"

Ralf's jaw dropped and banged against his neck.

With a flourish of supra-spacial iridescent light, a figure appeared beside him. It was Gwer Weyn, Possessor of Evrlife.

"Right, so where's that five bob you owe me?"

"What five?" asked Ralf.

Weyn triangled his arms, hands on his hips, then abruptly extended his open left hand, expectant as a Kduimlian in its twelfth trimester.

"Don't gimme that. Get on with it!"

Ralf pulled a fiver from his back pocket and handed it over.

Weyn nodded.

"Now down to business."

Weyn motioned for Ralf to join him in a seated position atop a small crate.

"What's been going on?" asked Ralf.

Weyn thought for a moment.

"Six hundred and thirty-two air tram pile-up on Air Route 3 over New West York; the Baystar Grits seceded from the League of Galactic Video Game Players to form a troupe of itinerant entertainers, something about expanding the boundaries of finger gymnastics; Elvina Clotwisz celebrates her forty-third marriage, to her manicurist this time; the Bureau of Investigation into Governmental Corruption was dissolved as its leaders were found to be involved in green slavery; Senator Tetraham announced his intentions to-"

"No no. I mean with you! This Evrlife thing. What have you been doing? It must be terribly exciting!"

"Well, yes." Weyn avoided Ralf's glance. "Actually, for the most part, so far, up to this point, you know, the majority of the work has been, actually, in reality..."

"Yes?" encouraged Ralf.

"Someone's got to do the paperwork! Anyhow, I've come to tell you something of extreme importance."

"Like?"

"Like, you know that guy they pulled out of the artifact?"

"Yeah..."

"He's not who he says he is. He's somebody else entirely," warned Weyn.

"That follows logically. If he's not who he says he is, then he's bound to be somebody else entirely. He'd have to be somebody else entirely. He could hardly be somebody else partially. I don't think they had limb transplants in his time."

Weyn stared at Ralf. "You want to hear this?"

"I'm all ears."

"I wasn't going to bring up the subject of your looks, Ralf."

Ralf stared at Weyn without reacting. "Something of extreme importance, you said?"

"Not yet I haven't said."

"Feel free to say it now, then."

"Right. You've got something important to do, Ralf."

"So I've heard. What would you be referring to?"

"An opportunity! A chance for daring, courageousness, the thrill of triumph, and the accomplishment of an immortally acclaimed deed!"

Ralf's eyes lit with excitement. "You mean Itez is

finally gonna let me be Mustard Boy for his Volleyfrankfurter team??"

"Better than that. You will bring truth to billions of mislead Alliance citizens. Remove the illusion and deception from their lives! Finally give them a chance to see reality as it really is!"

"So, enact tighter truth in advertising laws, and ban the packaging of merchandise in favour of the packing?"

"You been reading books again, boy?"

Ralf gave him his 'who, me?' look, and Weyn continued.

"No matter. That artifact? That Buck Rogers? Things are not as they appear."

"Oh?"

"Mmmm," grunted Weyn meaningfully. "I've uncovered an immense scandal. An audacious scheme. I've discovered that Aronism is based on the teachings of a false prophet. Jammy himself is a false prophet. An ordinary mortal with an insanely distorted ego. A hack philosopher believing himself the revealer of divine intent."

"How can you know that?"

"I was spoken to by the real deity of our universe. In a dream!"

"Oh well there you go. That proves it right there."

"Ralf," snarled Weyn. "Don't be flippant. I don't lie. And that's not the only evidence. There's a video that was found within the artifact. In it, this faker himself admits Aronism was just a scheme of his, meant to deceive!"

"Wow," stated Ralf, not looking at Weyn. He had found a salted Shurris Munchee gabanut in his pocket and was practising rolling it between his thumb and index finger. It's never too late, thought Ralf, to develop useful skills.

"And that's where you come in, Ralf!"

Ralf noticed the salt was coming off the gabanut and sticking to his index finger.

"It will be you who destroys the illusion, this Aron, that this faker has blinded us with for so long! It will be you who will destroy the false idol!"

Ralf shifted the gabanut to his other hand. He licked the salt off his index finger thoughtfully.

"Wouldn't that best be done by someone like, oh, a possessor of Evrlife?"

"No no, Ralf. I have my part to play in this too. The real Jammy, although that isn't his name, told me that this faker will come to you, and so it's up to you to set things straight."

Ralf threw the gabanut up into the air, tossed his head back, and opened his mouth.

"Don't worry Ralf. I don't lie, and when the time comes, I'll be there to help you do the right thing," Weyn continued his thought.

The gabanut lodged in Ralf's right nostril.

Weyn would have smirked had it not been for his body being blown away from under his face. Burned Zin remnants suddenly stained the far wall, and Berishu re-latched the safety on his vaser.

Chapter 17. Visions And Voices

Knuckles's life had come full circle. His religious/mystical experience, moments earlier drawn to an end, sat heavily in his mind; echoes of the knowledge and insight gained spread through his mind like cancer cells coursing through a recently healthy body, rapidly destroying a fragile equilibrium.

Unknown to his superiors on Mars, just over two sols earlier, when Knuckles had shed his mole skin as a radical Terran rights activist and severed his ties with the Covenant of the Sons of Aron sect, he had not shed all religious ideology. Below the fake skin of a Covenant Son, was the fake skin of a secular, martianistic public servant. Knuckles was a double mole.

When he dropped out of sight but then resurfaced a sol later as the dispassionately patriotic leader of the secret Alliance agency unknown as BOTCH, he had merely assumed another skin. Underneath the secular coating, he remained a religious zealot, albeit a more conventional one: a Martian Aronist who despised the Covenant Sons not only as a political menace, but as a religious affront.

Now he saw his true destiny, and the circle of his life had finally closed. Knuckles looked back on the wisdom with which he had turned his back on BOTCH by allowing the Supreme Purple Worm to bug his office.

He realized that these leaks of classified information had very likely weakened the Alliance and encouraged the Friggian attack on C-0004. If it hadn't been for the Friggians (along with the menagerie animals, plus a few killer celery) causing such mass chaos aboard the C-0004, the artifact would have been transported to Aqua Posteri 8 and officially lost. That would have sunk Knuckles's unexpected opportunity for personal growth.

Now, returning from the screening of the Aron video, and having read Clokene's report revealing the actual historical basis of Aron, Knuckles felt disillusioned with all his theological concepts. He had been alienated from Aronism, the religion that had shaped and guided him through the many stages of his life. He was a heathen not by his own choice. His belief had been involuntarily torn from his mental grip.

As Knuckles relaxed into a calm despair, the vision had come. A creature from beyond the confines of martian existence, all-knowing, infinitely powerful, well-dressed, shrouded in a veil of immense will and life-affirmation: a god. Not Aron, not an orthodox mythic god, but a new, palpably real and true god.

The vision spoke to him, gave him bearing for his currently adrift life. The new god explained that Aron had been a transient Terra/Mars chimera, a false icon from the age of illusion. Now was the time for truth to be heralded unto the people. Knuckles would enlist one more disciple into the new faith, one who would have the power to destroy the Aronist illusion and thus usher in an era when enlightenment would rule the infinite cosmos, one who would perform this deed efficiently and yet humbly, that is, if he could get the gabanut out of his nose.

=

Three or four seconds after Berishu pulled the activation stud on his vaser, the splattered Zin fragments that had previously composed Gwer Weyn shimmered into nothingness. No trace of the pirate remained. Evrlife was nothing if not tidy.

Another figure sparkled into existence beside Berishu, and Ralf and Berishu were introduced (correctly, this time) to Terry Aaronstrum, the perpetrator of the Alliance's favourite theological illusion. Niceties, names, and a handshake, along with a little excess gabanut salt, were exchanged.

Terry had disappeared from the secure medical bay (with some help but no explanation from Adept who was now nowhere to be seen) and then found himself amid the scattered cartage of the cargo deck. In unfamiliar territory, he recognized and instinctively trusted the innocent, friendly, and arguably juvenile look of Ralf.

Berishu explained it might be well to Terry's advantage to leave C-0004 at any time in the near if not immediate future. Terry hinted that, perhaps, with his new colonel rank in Space Corps, Ralf might be able to arrange a little something in the way of transportation.

Ralf considered this. Realizing his admiration for and wish not to annoy Captain Berishu, er, okay, Thom, and his immediate liking for the charismatic Aaronstrum, he felt compelled to provide that assistance.

Ralf shrugged humbly and offered to walk them to the nearest space taxi stand.

They answered his offer with uncertain glances to the floor, their watches, and each other. Guessing that the magnanimity of his offer might have embarrassed them to the point of refusal, Ralf assured them that it would be no trouble whatsoever, and that he wasn't busy at the moment anyway. With only minor additional amounts of uncertain foot shuffling, they accepted.

Chapter 18. Something Wicked This Way Thumps

C ommodore Trook paced the floor of her Space City's Control Centre, stopping her compulsive rolling only long enough to feed another organic vapour emission into the translator.

"Hipdip!" the Commodore's translator shouted at her second-in-command. She was not insulted, however, as this was her name. "News on the latest celery advances?"

"Not beautiful, Captain. Theta and Gamma Sections have fallen to the celery. Delta Section is rampant with menagerie animals. Friggians have taken the starboard computer annex along with Kappa Section. They are now engaging our forces in battle along one side of Lambda Section," was what Sub-Commodore Klick Hipdip's translator emitted.

"Ma'am!" interrupted a young technician, with both urgency of youth and nearing of shift end tight in his voice. "I've a visual from Sigma Section!"

Klick transferred the visual data to the main viewing screen. On the left side of the screen, the band of carnivorous celery advanced. Their insidious green stalks bobbed widely as they moved forward. On the right side of the screen, a large assortment of exotic animals roared, snarled, chirped, and hissed along their maddened charge.

"I don't believe it," muttered Klick's translator, as she buzzed furiously.

"I never really believed it could happen. At least, not in my lifetime!" complained the technician.

Trook shook the uppermost part of her body and re-plugged her translator input tube before it said: "Who would have thought. The Ultimate Confrontation of

Nature, the Apocalypse of Animal versus Vegetable, and it happens on my watch!"

Klick buzzed in despairing flippancy. "It was obvious that the vegetables would revolt. It's just I never thought it would be the celery. I mean, they're always been our friends," said her translator.

"Yes, I agree with that." Trook shook a top tentacle. "If it had been the potatoes, or maybe the tomatoes, then perhaps I could accept it. But to think! The celery!"

Trook, Klick, and the technician all shook their heads, pursed their lips (or whatever surrounded their various alien oral orifices), and stared helplessly at the view screen.

The two groups of entities, the celery and the animals, met at the center of the screen. Flesh and metal-augmented plant tissue flew. The computer automatically scanned the audio and instantaneously provided ragged little text balloons over each interaction reading 'biff!', 'whump!' and 'chomp!' at the appropriate moments.

The technician glanced at the clock mostly.

=

"Celery!" screamed Ralf.

"Uh, no, but I think I've got some radishes though," Terry dug deep into his pants pocket.

"I meant killer celery!!" Ralf pointed behind them where a two-meter-high, greenish corrugated vegetable stalk had crept up.

They froze.

It froze.

They turned and ran. Nobody likes frozen vegetables.

It thawed in a hurry and gave chase, emitting a continuous rasping growl. Having no vasers, their possible avenues of action were limited to: one, run; two, stop and make friends; or three, engage in hand-to-stalk combat. Having no idea what the killer celery's personal interests, religious, political or social convictions were, they feared that any attempt to make friends would end in something closely resembling miserable failure, or brunch.

The third alternative was closed to them as none had any experience in hand-to-stalk combat, except marginally Berishu who had once roughed up a sentient cornstalk during an intoxicated stupor while enjoying shore leave on Alderbaran Toodashate.

And so they ran. They ran down a corridor. They ran up a corridor. They ran down another corridor.

Occasionally as they ran, they would pause for a fraction of a second and try to open a portal. Of course, the inhabitants of the residential area they were running through always kept their doors locked to prevent burglaries and minimize the possibility of people escaping killer celery. And so they continued running. Up more corridors, down more corridors.

They ran past the open entrance of a cinema. Strains of the theme to 'The Return of the Lewd Potato Chip' filtered into the corridor.

They ran around the corner. Ralf palmed his emergency fire exit access key (given to all Space Corps Officers as a merit award after they learn to tie the devilishly complex Ejsaanon's Intestine knot) and opened the fire exit into the cinema.

Berishu and Terry hurried through, and Ralf slammed the door. Realizing his mistake, Ralf fumbled for the key again, opened the door, and himself entered. Then slammed the door again. The time for the Final Confrontation of Martianoid versus Vegetable had been slightly delayed.

"Down in front!" screamed a popcorn-stuffed mouth.

Ralf, standing onstage in front of the cinema screen, looked towards the voice, but his vision was impaired by the darkness of the cinema interior. Behind him, the plot of the 'Return of the Lewd Potato Chip' unfolded.

Ralf startled with a sudden realization: he had just saved over eighteen space bucks.

"Get down Ejsaanon lickers!!" screamed another popcorn-stuffed mouth.

Berishu, Terry, and Ralf stood peering uncertainly into the darkness for three seats together for a few seconds before they realized they were not alone on the stage.

A tall figure, faceless through the use of a black over-sized hood, and bodyless through the use of a black over-sized cape, stood next to a burly figure with shaggy black hair and arbitrarily semi-trimmed facial hair.

Ralf immediately recognized the latter as Gwer Weyn, possessor of Evrlife.

"Ralf!" Weyn stepped towards Ralf. "I've been looking for you."

"Didn't you get shot?" mused Ralf, not completely surprised. He was getting used to bumping into people whose deaths he had assumed.

"That's right," agreed Weyn.

"Well?"

"Yes, shot quite well, thank you." Weyn flicked the end of his thumbnail off his teeth at Berishu.

"So you're not dead?"

"Don't you listen, Ralf!? What were you doing in the Chamber of the Incomprehensible? Catching gabanuts with your nose?? Remember Evrlife? Eternal life and seven powerful powers?"

"Shut up and sit down!" screamed yet another popcorn-stuffed mouth.

Weyn drew his vaser and fired randomly into the audience. Screams and tumult resulted.

"Now, Ralf, have you thought about what we talked about last time, or has that slipped your, uh, mind also?"

"I've thought about many things since last we talked."

"Ralf," sighed Weyn as he crossed his arms over his chest. "Why don't you just level with me?"

"What?"

"I know the responsibility is too great for you. Just because you haven't got the guts to carry out what is right and necessary, doesn't mean you're totally worthless."

"What do you mean?"

"Look, okay, maybe you failed in destroying the false prophet, but at least you brought him here for me to deal with."

"Who is this idiot?" asked Berishu.

Weyn looked first at Berishu, then Ralf. "Surely you two have been introduced..."

Berishu's eyes remained on Ralf, his eyebrows slowly climbing towards a distant hairline.

"Captain Berishu, most excellent Space Corps Captain," said Ralf, "meet Gwer Weyn, ex-Zin pirate, possessor of Evrlife and the seven powerful powers."

"Glad to meet you," said Berishu as he extended his hand in a feint, then snatched Weyn's vaser, flicked off its safety, and plasmized the Zin into several wet chunks that hit the viewing screen with a sound like Jello being dropped thirty meters onto concrete. Many popcorn-stuffed mouths wailed in frustrated anger.

The tall hooded figure opened its mouth as if to speak but, before it had the chance, it faded into nothingness. The chunks of Zin corpse disappeared simultaneously.

Chapter 19. Space:1969

Terry, Berishu and Ralf didn't quite made it to the space taxi stand. Only thirty meters short of their destination, they were intercepted by City security forces. Their odds were poor: fifteen to three, that is, fifteen well-armed, extensively trained and brain-loaded fighters against one slightly out-of-shape but armed StarCraft, er, CargoShip ex-Captain, one musician with combat experience only in Tai-Pom-Doh (an ancient form of Terran forest combat using only the earlobes and certain parts of the scalp), and an underweight Terran with a successful background in the impromptu sprint.

If I had one more charge cassette for my vaser, Berishu figured, I'd go for it. As it was, they could only surrender. With thirty weapons of imminent death trained upon them, the three stood in a neat triangle: Terry and Berishu out front, Ralf behind.

As two of the apprehending force moved towards their triangle, Terry took a step away from its calming geometry.

So they had done it, he thought, unsettled. They had finally captured the dreaded Anti-Aron, me. Well, what will it be? Upside-down crucifixion, burning at the stake, or stoning?

Terry took another step away from his companions, not wanting to implicate them in his grave ecclesiastic misdeeds.

The two security officers shoved Terry aside and grabbed Ralf. One elbowed him sharply in the gut. Ralf promptly and loudly emptied his lungs with a wet cough of acquiescence.

"Prisoner subdued," announced the officer.

"And what..." Ralf gasped for some more air. "...am I being arrested for this time?"

The security officer with the biggest cluster of brass on his shoulder stepped towards Ralf.

"You were on Cavalesii 2 on or about 1968.006?"

"Um..." Ralf put the middle of his bent index finger to his lower lip. "Was that a Thursday?"

The officer denied him an immediate answer, and instead pulled out an very old and scarred data pod with the official Space Patrol insignia stamped in gold relief upon it. The electro-gold shimmered in the narrow spectrum lighting of the corridor as he brandished it.

"Captain Siso Sbor has supplied us with this document." The officer leaned in close to Ralf's face. "Do the words Andre's Parking Mall and Skin Care Boutique mean anything to you?"

"There was a quarter in the meter! I swear it!!"

"Yes," The officer pointed a menacing finger at Ralf. "But you didn't turn the handle."

Upon this revelation, a few of the other officers mumbled grimly to each other and cast dirty looks at Ralf.

"Ha!" A vengeful shriek came from behind Ralf. Both he and the nearest security officer flinched. "I spent two days scanning data from the central Alliance computer! But, at last, you are revealed for the rampant disregarder of noble Alliance statutes that you are!" snarled Captain Sbor.

She strode forward as a conquering warrior. Her moment of moral clarity was assembling.

Commodore Trook rested smugly beside Sbor, her top tentacles draped nonchalantly over her curvaceous apex.

"I hope I've got an extra bottle of shampoo at home," Berishu asided to Terry.

Terry shrugged his shoulders. "Why?"

Berishu nodded towards the viewport just behind Terry. A pale yet fully round orb shone against the starscape: Luna. Berishu's nostril hairs darkened. His earlobes disappeared and he began to take off his clothes.

"Isn't streaking still illegal in the 25rd century?" asked Terry, experiencing for the nth time his own unique form of cultural shock.

Berishu smiled as he began to sprout hair on his neck, hands, and feet. And back. And more on his chest. And more on his legs. And, okay, it was hurricane of hirsute erupting over his entire body.

The security officers began to check their watches, hoping against all perception of time passage that their shift had ended moments earlier. It hadn't.

Berishu, or the upright wolf that now stood in Berishu's place and carried his Space Corps ID, pilot license, social reassurance chip, and a Country Lanes Bowling Club gift certificate (even though the wolf would be unlikely to find bowling shoes in size twenty two), let out a practice howl. It wasn't his best, but several of the security officers checked their watches again anyway.

The wolf, then obviously demonstrating its displeasure with bowling shoe manufacturers, picked up the nearest security officer, aimed her carefully at the other officers and pitched. The wolf achieved a split, but still howled in disappointment.

"Too much spin," translated Ralf to the head security officer, who smiled condescendingly then ran for the exit.

The wolf ran to Sbor, threw its head back and howled really quite decently for only the third attempt.

"Indecent exposure, assaulting a peace officer, disturbing the peace, not wearing proper bowling shoes," Sbor ticked the misdeeds off on her right hand.

Suddenly and without warning... they came from the depths of unknown space. Three hundred and eleven canisters of nuclear waste cast out by a lesser empire. The abandoned chunks of ancient alien radioactive mass struck the Space City like a barrage from an interstellar tommy gun. Shredded chunks of exotech living accommodations were tossed into the solar winds. Sections of the immense engineering feat belched air into the void. Support systems overloaded and exploded, turning the orderly city into an arsonist's blazing delight.

The impact knocked out the artificial gravity only momentarily, causing Ralf, Sbor, and well, everyone to lose their balance and fall to the deck.

In the midst of the fiery chaos, Ralf and Terry crawled to a lift car. The security officers continued to play 'un-blind wolf's non-bluff' with Berishu's hairy transformation.

At that moment, a battalion of Friggian soldiers burst into the section. As you may recall, they were being chased by a group of exotic zoo animals battling mechanized carnivorous celery.

Sbor was frantically shaking the misbehaving Cavalesii 2 parking ticket data pod, and demanding the local security officer give her directions to an emergency uplink point.

Trook, already distraught about her command being reduced to a smouldering mass of wreckage for obscure, if not perhaps nonexistent reasons, was sure she was losing her mind. In the midst of the blazing pandemonium was a martianoid, no, an upright wolf, dancing with dramatic swoop and flourish, and playing the violin.

Chapter 20. My Least Favourite Martian

Terry and Ralf careened through the mass destruction, running underneath dangling cables that issued showers of sparks, and past the twisted and charred piles of steel sheets and polystyrene support beams that used to be the frame of the City, until they reached the landing platform inside Hangar 51 where the PLASMIC SURFER was parked.

They would have boarded the PLASMIC SURFER if it had not been for the distant voice that cried "Eh Ralf! Wait a second!!"

Thinking that perhaps something more important than escaping the imminent total decompression of the rapidly exploding Space City had turned up, Ralf stopped and waited for the owner of the distant voice to catch up to them. It was Knuckles.

"Hey, how's it going?" sallied Ralf.

Knuckles looked grim. "Ralf, there are things you must be made aware of. Things about the decisions you will have to make very shortly. Things about..."

Knuckles's sentence tapered off, mutating into an aggressively terrified glare at Terry.

"If this is a lecture about bad company," Ralf raised his shoulders in the first half of a shrug.

Knuckles put his hands on Ralf's shoulders and pushed them back down.

"Ralf, my friend, all my life I had been blinded by the ugly illusion of Aronism. My virtue bastardized by ignorance of True Godliness. All my life, that is, until a few hours ago."

Ralf attempted another shrug but Knuckles held his shoulders firmly down.

"This being you have with you is not what he appears to be. All these millennia, his false divinity has hidden the one true religion from the fair people of our

Alliance."

Gwer Weyn stepped out from black nothingness, and then aside to reveal a tall, faceless, hooded figure behind him. The three now faced Ralf and Terry.

"This is your chance, Ralf," Knuckles continued. "There is still time to right the wrongs of a thousand generations, still time to set straight the crooked path of ten thousand sols of foolish history. Step forward now, my friend, and accept Truth, Virtue, and the One Divine Path!"

Ralf turned to Weyn. "Gee, he sounds a lot like you when you finish a quest, all big numbers and odd capitalization."

"Listen not to his words, but his meaning, Brother in Enlightenment," chided Weyn.

Ralf considered attempting another shrug, but Knuckles had finally released his shoulders and he wasn't keen for a repeat engagement.

"This," Knuckles gestured to the hooded figure. "This is The Truth. This is what Aronism has hidden from us. Our true Master and Saviour from immortal melancholy and insignificance!"

"Hey," nodded Ralf to the figure.

"This is the ultimate guiding force to the eternal creation of our dynamic universe. Reveal thyself, Lord!"

Knuckles bowed to the figure, as did Weyn. The cloak and hood of the dark figure fell away. A tall, powerful-looking male martianoid stepped forward.

"Hi Jrrak," said Ralf.

"I am Jrrak, Great God of the Universe Tssarofentiasterogliss. I am here to declare my omnipotence and divinity. Of you whom will follow and worship me, I demand nothing- nothing but dedication to your Master and a pure heart in love for your God. In return, prosperity and order shall sweep in a new Age of Enlightenment!"

"Great!" smirked Terry. "Where do we vote?"

Weyn snarled wordlessly in Terry's direction.

"I don't understand," said Ralf. "What are you doing here, Weyn?"

Weyn corrected his posture and brought one of his arms across his chest, over his heart. "I am the Bringer of glad tidings, the Reaper of pure hearts."

"Because you're the possessor of Evrlife?"

"Mmmhmm, that's right."

"I thought Evrlife had something to do with being a crusader and warrior for joy, or something like that?"

"Right, well-"

"Those tests we had," Ralf turned to Jrrak "They didn't really test for inner beauty, did they?"

"What are you getting at Ralf?" asked Weyn.

"Well, I dunno, just, like, why didn't I get Evrlife, like, if I'm doing the right thing now, why wasn't I doing it then, and what did I do wrong, or like, uh,"

"Why didn't you get Evrlife?! Is that it, Ralf? Such vanity for a simple servant of my unimaginable Greatness!" admonished Weyn.

"Your what? I can't be, uh, have vanity?" Ralf frowned and raised his eyebrows simultaneously.

"An assumption!" Jrrak raised a finger at Ralf. "You said 'if I'm doing the right thing now'! Awake, O groveller before Destiny! Indeed, you are in danger! You are travelling a path perilous to your Eternal Spirit! This being who accompanies you, he is a Creator of Illusion! A Master of Lies! It is he who must be destroyed to allow enlightenment to permeate the cosmos!"

"But why Weyn and not me? I mean, I was a peaceful guy, and he ran around blowing up spaceships and doing Belaznian spores all the time!"

Weyn cleared his throat. "Now Ralf. I was an honourable Zin. I lived by the values of my culture and successfully guided others of my kind from my high status position. I was a true Zin pirate captain, and as such am of much value to beings of pure will, such as Jrrak, Great God of the Universe of Tssarofentiasterogliss."

"You were a loser!" countered Ralf.

"What did you say?" demanded Weyn.

"You were a failure! Your crew mutinied! And you mutinied the first time I met you!"

"I am the Divine Link! I am He who provides entry for the Great God Jrrak!" barked Weyn.

"Provides entry?" noted Terry softly.

"You know nothing! You shall condemn yourself to Eternal Damnation through your own ignorance! He who fails to destroy such a monstrosity as that!" Weyn pointed at Terry, "is no different than the evil he allows to propagate!"

"Uh, actually, Weyn," interjected Jrrak. "Ralf wasn't about to fail, that is-"

"You shall destroy yourself, Ralf," warned Weyn.

Terry stepped towards Jrrak and passed his hand through the space where the Great God stood.

"You know, Ralf, he ain't even here."

Ralf's eyebrows twitched. He was listening.

"I don't think he's anything at all,", continued Terry. "I think Weyn is 'the link' just like he admitted, and the only thing that Jrrak here," Terry began to imitate Jrrak's baritone voice, "the Great God of the universe of Tssarofentiasterogliss, has a hold of in our universe is Weyn himself."

Ralf's eyebrows twitched again.

"There is no Aron," stated Terry. "What do you say we keep it that way?"

"Foolish mortal!" bellowed Jrrak. "I am the ultimate in Pure Spirit. I am that from which you all came! It is only now that I unveil myself, and allow Truth to be known. My ways are mysterious, yet my Wisdom is all-knowing! Do not abandon your Virtue with foolish physical doubts and sins of ignorance! I am beyond that which is physical or what you might understand!"

"Beyond the physical?" mused Terry. "If I may quote a close friend of mine, 'there is no metaphysical sense, only metaphysical nonsense.'"

"Your friend? Adept is your friend? How is that possible?" started Ralf.

"He's Aron's original bass player," explained Terry patiently, "but, Ralf, let's leave something for the sequel, okay?"

Ralf shook his head, then stared hard at Jrrak. "You're not an Aron, and you are no Jammy."

"Enough chit-chat!" screamed Weyn, now pointing accusingly at Terry. "Destroy the viper! Kill the Anti-Aron!"

"Ralf, Aronism was but a cruel illusion of despair! Do not let True Faith be destroyed!" Knuckles pleaded.

"I have faith in Aron. That's Terry then really, isn't it, and he's a decent guy," argued Ralf.

"No no. You must not have Faith in a person. Faith is for Gods whose Divine Will is the simple definition of Correctness and Truth! I speak of Divine Faith!" cried Knuckles.

"Metaphysical faith? Like faith in what isn't really here like we are?" ventured Ralf.

"Kill the destroyer!" growled Knuckles.

Weyn withdrew his ceremonial Zin dagger from his belt and moved towards Terry.

"Uh-un!" yelled Ralf, as he stepped in between them.

Weyn batted him on the side of the head, and Ralf fell to the ground. Weyn smiled, ready to advance on Terry again, but Ralf grabbed one of the Zin's legs.

"Homely insect!" screamed Weyn as he tried to shake Ralf loose. Ralf bit the ankle hard, and Weyn toppled. They both scrambled to their feet. Weyn punched Ralf in the stomach, who then folded in on himself like a refilled stapler being closed.

"Halt!" cried Jrrak.

"Don't say that," pleaded Terry. "I like seeing people be honest."

Ralf punched Weyn on the elbow, spraining his own middle finger. Weyn did a flying Zin head-crusher knee lock onto Ralf. They fell to the floor again. Ralf screamed something that didn't sound much like a word. Weyn chuckled, and slammed Ralf's head against the deck.

Once. Twice.

Ralf hoped that Berishu did indeed have lots of shampoo back at the crate. Berishu would need a lot of suds to shampoo his wolfish hide, but Ralf would need an even more generous supply to get all of his own blood out of his hair.

Weyn grabbed Ralf's nose and used it as a handle to bring the semi-conscious head down hard against the floor for a third and final time.

A moment of silence, or two, and Weyn got up. Ralf didn't.

Weyn again advanced towards Terry, dagger drawn.

The ex-Zin Pirate saw red, and had a huge body-wracking orgasm. Then he saw green, and experienced an existential ecstasy of pure understanding. A strong black light strobe momentarily emptied his mind to a void calm. Other colours flashed by. Blue, yellow, purple, orange, they accelerated into a pure white, a maelstrom of emotional possibility. The physiological changes the Zin moved through would amaze the most weathered tri-galactic physician. A white brilliance became blinding, then melted away.

To Weyn, reality was now an anticlimactic inconvenience. He would not move. He could not think. Physiological depression ran rampant through his body.

Ralf shoved the small oblong device Adept had gifted him back into his pocket. He wiped some of his own blood from his hand onto his pant leg.

Jrrak screamed in useless rage. Reflected in Weyn's glazed-over eyes, Jrrak faded back to nothingness, or actually to Tssarofentiasterogliss.

"No!" wailed Knuckles. "I can't accept this. My religion, my faith, ripped from me a second time in one night!"

Terry smiled. "The second time is usually easier."

As Terry carried Ralf onto the PLASMIC SURFER, Ralf's hazy vision focused on the blood stains on his shirt.

"What kind of detergent do you use?" managed Ralf just before unconsciousness claimed him.

Chapter 21. A Well-Balanced Riot

When Berishu regained his martianoid form, the strategic situation on Space City C-0004 had tilted. Very few Alliance personnel remained on the station, and most of those were wounded, disoriented, in hiding, or absent from duty on account of short-notice stress leave.

Berishu climbed the emergency access ladder into the Control Centre. It was deserted.

His first order of business was to delete any surveillance images of his transformation into a ferocious bipedal wolf. Not even a Martian officer would be forgiven that type of aberration.

The recorded images showed several of his furry crimes. One was the decapitation of Captain Siso Sbor. Another involved eating a few crucial bits of Commodore Pob Trook. That was unlikely to have been tasty, mused Berishu, thankful for the usual amnesia during his transformations.

Second order of business was ascertaining the status of the Friggian boarding party. Berishu scanned the current data feeds from all remaining city sections. No Friggians onboard? Berishu adjusted the time locus back a few hours to review how the fighting had evolved. Soon it was clear.

The escaped zoo animals had encountered the carnivorous mechanized celery, stripped them of their armour and infogear, and then ingested them. Eating the vegetables only served to strengthen the rampaging animals, and they pressed on, fortified with essential vitamins.

As the menagerie escapees had approached the Friggian front, they continued to eat whatever was in their way, including in this case the atomic wastes from deep space that had momentarily disrupted the City's artificial gravity. After ingesting the highly radioactive substances, the animals began to mutate.

One reptile grew to an enormous size and jettisoned its normally staid personality in favour of a more maniacal approach to eating new life forms.

One turtle likewise grew, but then resisted eating a group of school children; instead it turned on its own kind and began battling the other now-enormous mutants, while the school children cheered it on.

The Friggians took note of the location of the school children, adjusted their weapons, and eradicated them with a volley of floater mines. This upset the giant turtle who fired up a built-in rocket drive that existed under its tail (who knew?), flew directly at the Friggians, and began to crush clumps of them in its multi-occupant jaws.

The other mutated animals followed the turtle's lead and were soon also chewing down large quantities of Friggians.

After that, little was left. Most of the City sections had been thoroughly destroyed. Only a few mutant zoo animals now wandered about Theta Section, tired and upset with indigestion.

Berishu remotely sealed the bulkheads between Theta Section and the rest of the city, then opened the airlocks.

The live video feed showed the final zoo animals exploding from the decompression. The battle for Space City C-0004 was over.

Twenty minutes later, the City was surrounded by an veritable armada of Space Corps warships.

=

In hyperspace, a day later, Ralf regained consciousness. Terry and Adept peered down at him and smiled.

"Relax, Ralf. You're on the PLASMIC SURFER. Luckily, Adept here knows how to fly this thing."

"Adept? Oh. What about Captain Berishu? Is he okay?"

Terry nodded.

"You mean Admiral Berishu, the hero who saved Space City C-0004 from the Friggians? He should be settling into his new corner office by now."

"Really? That's amazing considering he is a Terran, and the space city is actually round," said Ralf.

"Well, Adept here worked his magic on the secure Alliance data nets. It's amazing what you can do by just twiddling a few digital bits in a paperless society. You'd think you people would have learned something after that Great Reset. Also, Ralf, corner office is just an expression."

"So you really are a god? You really are the Jammy?" Ralf's eyes widened out to their usual near circularity.

Terry shook his head, but it was Adept who answered.

"I won't claim that, Ralf. Terry is just a human. Just like I am."

"A what?" Ralf was confused by the unusual word.

"Human. A Terran. An Earthling. We are both from ancient Earth. In fact, a famous ancient Earthling once said that any sufficiently advanced technology is indistinguishable from magic. Now I happen to have this strawberry-coloured alien acorn that does whatever I think I want it to do. I used to be a lot older, and in fact a bit shorter than I am now, so you tell me what's what. Am I a god? Was the alien who devised my magic acorn a god? Are all the other so-called gods we met travelling the galaxy actually deities, or just some jerks with similar acorns? Well, yeah, probably. So it maybe is a matter of a distinction without a difference."

"Uh huh," Ralf half-nodded, somewhat distracted as he was now recovered enough to scroll through the apps on the medical berth console.

"You have a long life ahead of you, Ralf," predicted Terry. "I hope you understand that whatever ideas you take on, and whatever people you cling to, these are the things that will determine your path through life.

Only these choices will determine if you are beautiful or ugly, and it is context-dependent; without ideas, or other people, we are a sum of zero. We can only ever be one, a unity, something that works together in harmony, if peace exists between all our parts. And this produces a joy based on true plurality, or a shared destiny of mutual values.

Therefore, you have to be careful when you join with others, because they are on their own arc, and it can be difficult seeing where that delivers them, and what they will be when they get there.

Don't get slipped off your own tentative purchase on reality by others veering in front of you, my young friend," advised Terry.

But Ralf was not paying attention. He had already recovered enough to sit upright and play a new round of Comets on the berth console.

=

They travelled undetected for several more days. It was on that trip that Ralf made a great personal discovery. Somewhere in his subconscious, the facts had been accumulating, slowly gelling into tangible shape. Throughout his adventures, unbeknownst to him, clues, probabilities, and tables of tendencies had been coalescing into solid conclusions.

One moment Ralf was staring at his thumbnail vacantly, and the next moment, the information presented itself to him as a thing complete, a series of postulations long ago tested.

"How could I have been so blind?" Ralf shook his head in wonder at the ineffable opacity of experience.

With a slow sigh of calm victory, he walked determinedly to the ship's rec center and mounted the

Mangle-A-Rabitt video game.

He grinned smugly, for now he realized that all one needed to do to score the special '10x Your Points' bonus was to spread toxic wastes on the carrot fields and pour cement down the rabitt holes before you mangled the last rabitt! It was almost too easy.

They left the PLASMIC SURFER in orbit around the planet Carnal Valle, the pleasure and leisure center of the Alliance. Ralf promised to write regularly, and they parted ways: Terry and Adept to find their true destiny, or at least a decent bar gig, and Ralf, well, Ralf took the inter-system econo-shuttle back to Mars.

Chapter 22. The Martian In The High Castle

R alf did not expect a Martian reception of well-wishers and free transportation, but as he exited the econo-shuttle amid a stream of banapple farmers on off-season sojourn and non-Martian students returning for the autumn quarter-sol semester, he noticed a martianoid female holding a sign with his name on it.

Curious, he approached her.

She dropped the sign before he could speak, and embraced him. Then he felt a pinch on his neck, and lost consciousness.

=

When Ralf regained consciousness, he was lying on a very soft bed, in a sumptuous hotel suite, facing the famous face of Sir Phuddel, the most powerful politician in the Alliance.

"Welcome to Mars, Ralf!" exclaimed Sir Phuddel in a decidedly friendly manner.

"What happened?" Ralf felt very groggy, despite not having ingested any grog. "Why did you drug me, and bring me here?"

"Relax Ralf, you're in fine company. We didn't want you to go through all that rush hour traffic fully conscious, that would be cruel." Phuddel patted Ralf's upper arm reassuringly. "But, alas, we do have some very sad news for you. Your father, our dear friend Agmewobbi, Agmewobbil, um, dear Agme, our Ultimate Senator for this last sol..."

"Is he here? Does he want to congratulate me?" asked Ralf, clearly not registering the words 'very sad'.

"He had arrived at C-0004 just before the major problems began. He'd heard about your promotion to Colonel, and wanted to congratulate you," lied Phuddel.

"Really? He didn't show up at my graduation, and I

haven't seen him for nearly two whole sols! They say it was security issues. Does that make any sense?" demanded Ralf, a little loose of inhibition due to the lingering effects of the sleepy drugs.

"Of course, of course. The terrible, ugly, sad truth is that Agme lost his life in the Friggian attack. He died a hero, certainly."

"He's dead?" asked Ralf, his head now a riot of incomplete sentences.

"A great loss that we shall all miss," dissembled Phuddel. "On the day he was killed, he was getting ready to sign an agreement with the Supreme Purple Worm that would've safeguarded the Alliance's future. It was a cabal of Friggians and Terra-first Aronists who plotted his death, you know. Now, you have the chance to make it right, to take on his job as Ultimate Senator, and sign the agreement yourself."

"Uh?" Ralf was dumbfounded that he would be considered to take the place of his father, a parent so devoutly dedicated to the Alliance that he apparently had little time for family.

"Yes, Ralf. This free trade agreement with the domain of the Supreme Purple Worm will ensure a balance of power in the tri-galactic area. The Friggians will have no choice but to withdraw."

Ralf signed the agreement, and dozed off.

Twenty minutes later, the Martian Stock Exchange gained twenty percent, and some from the Worm domain descended to the surface of Terra to began to eat its crust.

The Martian press called it right-sizing the crust, and noted that crust was the part of bread viewed as least attractive by mainstream martianoids. Some Terra-related stocks dropped sharply, but this had little impact on the overall economic performance of the Alliance that quarter.

Chapter 23. Closing Time

A day and a half later, Ralf sat in a New West York bar contemplating his life, so far. The position of Ultimate Senator had been revealed to be a telecommute job with little responsibility. Sometimes he had to sign papers, but generally didn't have to get out of his pajamas to do so.

With all the extra time my new and very comfortable government job affords, thought Ralf, I can finally focus on the big picture and make a difference for society.

Ralf took an introductory sip of his beer, only to find it unappealingly warm.

"You wouldn't have some ice cubes for this?" he called to the bartender.

"I'll pretend I didn't hear that!" growled the greasy biped.

"Right. Why is it so dead in here anyway?" Ralf asked, looking about at the sparse population of the dimly lit space.

"Brain worms. Don't you get the news?"

"Not really. Not a follower," replied Ralf.

He chugged the remains of his ambient, foamy tipple and slapped the appropriate amount of currency on the bar.

From the far end of the bar, an attractive Martian female named Sue E. Generous eyed Ralf as he stood. She had been hired by BOTCH to honeypot the new Ultimate Senator, but was biding her time.

Stepping into the street, Ralf's eyes wandered upward, scanning the deep black Martian night sky.

He looked out among the tiny bits of distant stellar fire that represented so much, and his thoughts strayed to the truly important things in the greater All.

As he peered into that infinite, hostile yet tender,

sad yet sprightly, frightening yet awe-inspiring void that lay above the Martian atmosphere, he thought of the adventures that awaited him… the wine, the women, the song, the sugar annuli, perhaps another ride on that anti-gravity space scooter, looking down upon the lights of Valle Martiana, floating serenely a dozen megameters above, or even the next release of Comets which promises to have multi-elemental out-gassing, in short, all the things that made life worth living.

Maybe, someday, he would have a chance to explore all the experiences that life, reportedly, could offer.

Ralf considered these possibilities and then pondered his humble beginnings. Or were they humble? Come to think of it, I can't remember my beginnings at all, thought Ralf. Maybe the beer hadn't been watered down after all.

He contemplated this thought for only a brief moment, as he realized just how implausible it was.

The dark was not cold tonight. Ralf drew a deep breath of the fresh night air, warm as a newly baked muffin, and the grim universal isolation, yes, the inevitably grim universal isolation of intelligent life everywhere was not his again.

"And why is this?" queried Ralf softly of himself. Why should I be different, or am I? And why should I care, or do I?

Did others have some personal stake in this, the matter of my place in the essence of the All?

Ralf was unsure. But surely the son of Agmewobbialluyllsesmeecolysion should not be concerned with such things. Or should he? What should he be concerned with, then? Ralf was not sure. Or was he? Were any of the others sure? Or weren't they?

These were and are the immortal questions of the universe, Ralf thought. Someday, he swore inwardly, he would answer all of them. Or at least some of them.

Or possibly a few. Ralf thought, will I or won't I? This, at least, I must discover!

He continued to consider these questions, and this was beautiful, as they are important questions.

Acknowledgements

The author would like to acknowledge
and thank those authors and creators
who inspire him, including but not
limited to:

Douglas Adams, Sylvia & Gerry
Anderson, Isaac Asimov, Ben Bova,
Ray Bradbury, Arthur C. Clarke, Philip
K. Dick, Stephen R. Donaldson, Harlan
Ellison, Rob Grant, Harry Harrison,
Robert A. Heinlein, Doug Naylor, Larry
Niven, Frederik Pohl, Gene
Roddenberry, Robert J. Sawyer, and
Robert Silverberg.

Dear Reader,

Thank you for purchasing this book.
If you enjoyed reading it, and would
like to read the next instalment in the
series, please consider leaving a
positive review on a website such as
Amazon, GoodReads, Chapters, *etc.*